S.C.R.E.A.M.

THE MUMMY'S REVENGE

ANDREW BEASLEY

USBORNE

DANGER UNWRAPPED

For eternity I wish to sleep,
This deadly curse I vow to keep.
For those who dare disturb my tomb,
Remember you have sealed your doom!

The words spun round and round inside Douglas McCrimmon's head. Just thinking about the mummy's curse made the young lad shiver beneath his uniform, as if a clammy hand was tracing a finger slowly down his spine.

Douglas, "Doogie" to his friends, knew that it wasn't his place to speak out. He was a servant, and the first rule of being a servant was *Hold your tongue*. Well, that and *Do as you're told*. So Doogie said nothing and kept pouring the drinks. All around him people were eating sandwiches from silver trays and drinking champagne, laughing and joking without a care in the world. But with every glass that Doogie filled, he stole another glance at the looming shape of the sarcophagus at the far end of the great hall.

An upright box. An ancient coffin. *With a monster inside.*

Doogie rummaged in his waistcoat pocket for a crumpled square of card. He'd sneaked one of the invitations and although he had read it a hundred times he still couldn't believe it.

Sir Gordon Balfour

At home

November 30th

44 Morningside Place

A mummy from Egypt to be unwrapped at 2.30 p.m.

Refreshments from 2.00 p.m.

What kind of numptie thinks that's a good idea?

But if Sir Gordon was worried, he didn't show it. With a red fez balanced on the top of his head, like a cherry on a bun, Sir Gordon was having fun. The great and good of Scottish society crowded round him; lords, ladies and gentlemen. *Tell us again about the pyramid… We must hear more about the tomb…*

Doogie took a sideways look at Mr Cowley. As always, the old butler was the calm at the centre of the storm. Strong and silent as stone – his angular face might have been carved from Edinburgh granite. Unflappable, unmoveable. Not one grey hair out of place. Doogie flashed the butler a quick smile, hoping for reassurance, but Mr Cowley didn't show even the merest flicker of emotion. Even so, Doogie was certain that Mr Cowley felt the same way he did – *Sir Gordon would bring the mummy's curse down on them all.*

Doogie weaved his way between the guests, edging across the tiled floor until he was close enough to hear what Sir Gordon was saying.

"I cannot think of anything worse than leaving a mummy in the sand to rot…" said Sir Gordon.

I can, thought Doogie. *Bringing the evil thing home!*

When Sir Gordon had first announced that he was going on an expedition to Egypt, it had sounded so mysterious and daring. However, the servants hadn't got too excited – they were used to Sir Gordon's enthusiasm for new hobbies, and how quickly those pastimes were put back on the shelf when the next thing came along.

Sir Gordon had filled his enormous house with every new gadget and invention that money could buy. In the last three years alone he had been absolutely passionate about photography, then British wildlife and finally exotic insects, all of which had been pursued wholeheartedly…for about five minutes.

Doogie remembered when Sir Gordon purchased a camera, the most expensive on the market, naturally. His Lordship didn't use it to capture scenes of the beautiful Scottish Highlands or formal pictures of his family and friends. Oh no, Sir Gordon only took *post-mortem* pictures; photographs of the dead, which he had framed and displayed in his study.

Sir Gordon's interest in animals was equally odd. He preferred them dead, so that he could stuff them, dress them up like people and arrange them in glass cabinets. He had squirrels playing cards, a rabbit on a miniature bicycle and a badger smoking a pipe.

Sir Gordon's insect and arachnid collection on the other hand was very much *alive*, mostly poisonous and almost entirely terrifying. Sir Gordon had spoken of nothing but tarantulas and scorpions for nearly two months before he got bored and never mentioned them again. Cowley still had to clean the glass tanks and feed them dead mice though. Sir Gordon insisted that only his faithful butler could be trusted to look after his pets. Come to think of it, Sir Gordon made it clear that Mr Cowley was the *only* man for quite a lot of things around the house. Certainly the poor old butler got all the rotten jobs.

The way Mr Cowley described it, Sir Gordon's new Egyptian hobby was basically grave robbing, although the graves were in another country and the bodies were very old, so that made it archaeology or something. Whatever it was called, Doogie had been amazed by the enormous hoard of treasures that Sir Gordon had brought home from the desert. Naturally it was Cowley who'd had to painstakingly label and catalogue each item, arrange and clean and polish them, then position the gas lamps so that they might be seen in their full glory.

Still, the effect was breathtaking.

The ballroom of 44 Morningside Place had been transformed into a private museum, and the whole chamber gleamed with gold. All around Doogie there were statues and burial masks and curved swords and bracelets and amulets and brooches and jars and...the list went on.

"I'm overjoyed that these marvellous objects didn't

stay buried in Egypt, just gathering dust," Sir Gordon continued, his pink sweaty face beginning to shine like boiled ham, "but instead were brought here, to *my* house, for all my dear friends to enjoy."

There was a lot of *oohing* and *ahhhing* at this point as everyone paused to appreciate the ancient artefacts which surrounded them on every side.

Like magnets, Doogie's eyes were once again drawn to the burial casket at the far end of the hall. It stood there like a soldier on guard; unmoving and yet filled with the potential for danger. An Egyptian coffin. Complete with a dead Egyptian inside.

Three other mummies were arranged beside it. A baboon, a cat and a baby crocodile. They made Doogie go all shoogly inside with dread.

Mr Cowley had told Doogie all about mummies – he was an absolute expert. Thousands of years ago, when a rich Egyptian died, he had his body preserved so that he could live again. It was a long and horrifying process. As Doogie understood it, all of the bits inside the body were taken out and saved in special jars, then the hollow body was filled with cotton, a lot like Sir Gordon's poor stuffed animals. Oils were rubbed on the skin to keep it from drying out and then the body was wrapped from head to toe in bandages, before the boiling hot *mūm* – sealing wax – was poured on. The whole idea terrified Doogie…but at the same time it excited him just a little bit too. Perhaps it was the same for Sir Gordon?

Sir Gordon called for quiet, banging a cake fork against his glass. Men in tweed jackets and women in ostrich feather hats jostled, ever so politely, for the best position to view the unwrapping.

Sir Gordon tapped too vigorously. The glass shattered.

"Dear friends," said Sir Gordon, as Doogie stepped in to take the broken glass from his hand, "some of you might know about my death-defying exploits in a distant desert land. Last year I led an expedition to a secret location in the desolate waste of the Theban Hills, beneath the mountainous shadow of the peak of *al-Qurn* – 'the Horn'…" Sir Gordon's voice trembled like a bad actor's. "There I was, in the great Valley of the Kings, the sun burning down on my head, the sand blistering my feet, the vultures circling endlessly above…"

"Oh no, not this old story again," one of the guests whispered too loudly. "I know for a fact he never left his hotel."

"Anyway, enough about me and my brilliance," Sir Gordon continued, pretending he hadn't heard.

"Let's get this chappie out and have a look at him, eh?"

An expectant hush fell. No one moved. Doogie could feel his own breath trapped inside his chest in anticipation. Sir Gordon grinned like a schoolboy who's been given the key to the sweet shop. The great hall was as silent as the grave…

Then they heard the knocking. Three loud raps.

Tap. Tap. Tap.

The crowd gasped and started to shuffle uncomfortably. *Where was it coming from?*

TAP! TAP! TAP! The knocking came again. Louder, more insistent this time.

It couldn't be…could it?

In spite of the mass of bodies in the hall, the temperature suddenly seemed to drop. Impossibly…terrifyingly… the sound was coming from the sarcophagus itself. As Doogie watched, the coffin lid shifted a fraction. Something inside wanted to get out.

Instantly Sir Gordon's guests were wide-eyed and sober; fear ran cold in their veins. The sarcophagus was opening in front of them. Inch by inch it was being pushed open…*from the inside.* One woman with an enormous bottom – and an even more enormous bowl of trifle in her hand – wobbled, and before anyone could catch her, she fainted to the floor. The bowl shattered; trifle went everywhere.

"Stay calm," Sir Gordon mumbled. "It's just gas that has built up inside the casket. Yes, that must be it…" He tried to convince himself. "The warm air in the room has reacted somehow with the air inside and—"

The lid opened further with a terrible screech. Sir Gordon took a step backwards as a foul stench poured into the hall.

"Just gas… I'm only moving backwards in case the body explodes…"

Doogie retched – the smell was worse than cleaning out the toilets. All around the hall the guests began to gag as their nostrils were filled with a stink more disgusting than rotting vegetables, putrid fruit, overripe cheese and decaying fish. Like the worst fart imaginable; silent but deadly.

A gentleman removed his hat and, with as much dignity as he could muster, vomited into it.

There was a gasp from the crowd as a bandaged hand appeared around the edge of the lid. The exposed tips of bone tapped against the stone as if the creature was impatient to be free.

That was when the screaming started.

No one was very polite now. There was no "Ladies first" or "After you, sir". This was every man for himself; a desperate, messy rush for the doors. Chairs were flung aside and tables upturned as people fled for their lives, stumbling and falling over each other in the chaos.

Only Sir Gordon, his butler and Doogie, stayed put; Mr Cowley no doubt out of a sense of duty, His Lordship possibly out of stupidity. Doogie could feel the hairs standing on end across the back of his neck. He was desperate to run away but his legs felt as if they had turned to lead.

The sarcophagus lid swung wide and the mummy almost fell into the room. The thing staggered on stiff, straight legs. It was wrapped in bandages from head to foot. But if the bandages had ever been white they were filthy now, like rags. And as the creature flexed its withered muscles, here and there more strips of cloth started to come loose, revealing horrible glimpses of the body inside.

The mummy lurched forwards and its knee joints squeaked as they were forced to bend for the first time in five thousand years. All the monster's movements were clumsy and awkward, like a newborn's. Although this creature wasn't a newborn; it was just the opposite: old and dead.

Doogie was still frozen to the spot, unable to move, or hide, or do anything other than stare. They were utterly alone: the boy, the butler, their master and the monster.

The mummy stumbled around like a drunk, but it seemed to Doogie that it was gaining strength with each passing second. The thing blundered into one of Sir Gordon's display cases, shattering the glass and sending the Egyptian amulets inside cascading down. The creature looked at one of the gold bracelets and paused, as if it was trying to remember something that had been very important many centuries ago.

Then it began to roar.

"Rrrrrrrrrrrrrgggggggggggggggggggggghhhhhhhhhhhhhhh!"

The sound was sudden and shocking, an angry animal noise which grew louder as the mummy started to rampage further through the room. With outstretched arms, it lashed furiously at the displays of Egyptian treasure…all the precious things that had been stolen from *his* tomb.

Sir Gordon and Mr Cowley clung to each other in terror while the mummy smashed the head off a statue with a final snarling roar, and then lurched towards the doorway. It was halfway out when it paused and turned its neck with a creaking sound, until it was gazing directly at Doogie.

Doogie might have been mistaken but it looked as if the mummy only had one eye.

It was either that, or the monstrous thing had winked at him.

CHAPTER ONE

"I WANT MY MUMMY!"

London was shrouded in fog. The gas lamps flickered in the streets, giving just enough light to make the shadows even scarier. All the ordinary, everyday folks were safely tucked up in their beds. But Charlotte Steel and Billy Flint were wide awake, in their secret headquarters. Beneath Westminster Abbey. In a crypt.

They were safe there, hidden from prying eyes. That was important, because what Charlotte Steel and Billy Flint did was anything but safe. And if the public knew what they were doing, then London, and the whole of Britain, might never be the same again. There would be

17

lots of screaming probably. Widespread panic. Wet pants. That sort of thing.

"The Supernatural Crimes, Rescues, Emergencies and Mysteries squad is not your typical police unit," Charley explained to their visitor.

"You can say that again," said Sir Gordon Balfour. The underground vault in which they sat was vast and echoing. As well as the tombs of long-dead knights and forgotten saints which Sir Gordon expected to find in the crypt of London's most famous church, there were also rows of wooden cabinets labelled alphabetically. Sir Gordon read some of the labels: *Abominations (various); Apparitions; Banshees; Bloodsuckers; Burrowers; Crawlers; Crypt spirits (clean); Crypt spirits (unclean); Darklings; Demons; Devil's footprints (sightings).* Sir Gordon's scalp itched and sweat broke out across his face in spite of the chill of the tomb. "Couldn't we have met in my club instead?"

"I thought you'd be right at home," chipped in Billy. "What with you being a famous archaeologist."

Sir Gordon squirmed a little in his seat. "My, er, role was more of a leadership position."

Charley raised an eyebrow. "Did you go into the mummy's tomb at all?"

"I was supervising."

"Sounds like hiding to me," sniffed Billy.

"I didn't come here to be made a fool of!" Sir Gordon protested, his podgy hands slamming down on the table.

"Where do you normally go?" asked Billy, all innocent. His grin dropped when Charley's small hard fist punched his leg under the table.

"Please ignore my partner, Sir Gordon," purred Charley, her educated voice ringing like fine crystal compared with what poured out of Billy's bucket mouth. "His whole family are criminals."

Billy shrugged, then wiped his nose on the back of his hand. "It's a fair cop, guv," he said. He gave Charley a wink. She gave him a glare.

"Trust me, Sir Gordon," Charley continued, unruffled. "We are professional detectives attached to the Metropolitan Police Force. If anyone can help you out of your…difficulties, S.C.R.E.A.M. can."

Sir Gordon appeared defeated, rather than convinced. He slumped lower in his seat, like a sulky child. There was a soft farting sound, which might have been the leather chair. "I am cursed," he said, his fleshy cheeks wobbling. "*Evil* has followed me home from Egypt. My every waking moment is clouded by the shadows of fear.

I cannot rest, I cannot eat, I cannot sleep. My stomach churns constantly—"

"I had a curry like that once," muttered Billy.

"Stop it," Charley mouthed.

Billy took a breath to say something else but a glance from Charley's clear blue eyes buttoned his lip tight. For now, anyway.

Billy Flint and Charlotte Steel couldn't have been more different. He was dark-haired, broad-shouldered, poor, and, if he was honest, common. Charlotte was none of those things, but their partnership worked. Some might describe them as chalk and cheese, but Billy knew better. He and Charley were more like spit and polish. And Charley Steel was definitely the polish.

"We truly appreciate you making the long journey down from Edinburgh to meet with us, Sir Gordon," said Charley. "But since we are the smallest department in the police force, you will understand that our resources are…modest."

"Hmmm," huffed Sir Gordon. "How many men do you have available for my case?"

"We will put our entire department at your disposal," Charlotte reassured him.

"Ten men? Twenty?"

It was Charlotte's turn to feel uncomfortable. S.C.R.E.A.M. had only three detectives. Charley Steel herself, Billy Flint and their leader, Luther Sparkwell – who at that precise moment was wearing a tatty dressing gown and was slumped face down at the table, apparently fast asleep.

"What you see is what you get, mate," said Billy.

"Three?" said Sir Gordon incredulously. "THREE! A peasant, a buffoon and a...a...girl!" It wasn't clear which he was most offended by.

Quite suddenly Luther Sparkwell lifted his head. His hair was wild and his expression wilder.

"Not just *any* girl," said Sparkwell. "A scientific genius with a flair for deductive reasoning and more learning in her little finger than you have in the shrivelled walnut you call a brain."

Sir Gordon harrumphed, but Sparkwell continued. "*I* am probably the country's leading expert on the arcane, the bizarre, all things paranormal and unexplained. And that 'peasant', as you so charmingly described him, is the best weapon we have in the fight against the supernatural."

Sparkwell paused for dramatic effect. "Billy is *sensitive*—"

"That doesn't mean I like kittens and cry when I graze my knee," said Billy quickly. "I'm sensitive to the spirit realm."

"My young friend has a gift," Sparkwell continued, his fingers twitching like an angry spider. "Billy can detect forces that are not of this world; he can track these entities back to their source. He can literally sniff out the sort of trouble that fools like *you* –" he aimed a pointed stare at Sir Gordon – "get yourselves into when you meddle with things that are best left alone."

Sir Gordon squirmed. "Well, I might have been a bit hasty," he mumbled.

"You might have been a bit dead!" said Sparkwell. "You have stolen relics which should have remained in their tomb never to be disturbed, you've incurred the wrath of ancient powers beyond your imagination, and you've released a creature over which you have no control. And we –" Sparkwell threw his arms out wildly – "a peasant, a buffoon and a girl, are your only hope!"

A heavy tear started to roll down Sir Gordon's plump cheek.

The room fell into an awkward silence, punctuated by the man's sobs.

22

"He's crying for his mummy," said Billy.

Charley pulled a face and gave Billy *the look.* Billy shrugged.

"You're right," Sir Gordon confessed, pulling himself together with a final trumpet-like blast into his handkerchief. "I need your help."

"So," said Charley, taking out a notebook and pencil. "Tell us everything you've done, you naughty boy."

CHAPTER TWO

THE SANDMAN

With a great hiss of steam and a scream of protest from the iron wheels, the Special Scotch Express hauled itself out of King's Cross Station. Charley and Billy sat opposite each other in their wood-panelled carriage. "Ten and a half hours, Duchess, and we'll be there," said Billy cheerfully.

Charley wasn't a real duchess, although her family *were* incredibly rich. Billy called her that affectionately. It annoyed her slightly, which was another good reason to do it. Charley pulled a tartan rug across her knees and gave him a glare, which quickly softened into a smile.

She looked every bit the young lady, Billy thought. Crisp white blouse, tweed jacket, a small silver fob watch strung like a pendant around her neck. Genteel, elegant, refined. But more fool anyone who thought that she was just some weak girl who needed looking after. Billy knew that Charley Steel had a tongue that could sting sharper than a wasp. And if that didn't work, there was always the pistol she had hidden beneath that blanket.

Sir Gordon was somewhere on the same train, they knew. But His Lordship was up the posh end in First Class, travelling with his butler and some other servants no doubt. Luther Sparkwell had stayed behind in London. Sparkwell had promised to join Billy and Charley when the case of the Hammersmith zombie had been solved. Even if Scotland Yard were too cautious to publicly mention the crimes that S.C.R.E.A.M. were involved with, it was a matter of professional pride that they always got their man. Or woman. Or, in some cases, *thing*.

That was where Billy's unique talents came into play. While the rest of his family were out robbing post offices, the young Billy had stayed at home and thought about monsters. Billy was different like that. Even as a child he'd had a connection to the paranormal realm. He could see invisible things and sometimes even talk with them too. There were ghosts in his street. And an angel at number twenty-two, and a demon, disguised as a very old man, living over the greengrocer's. Billy couldn't explain his skill, and he certainly couldn't control it. But it was definitely a very useful ability if your job was solving supernatural crimes.

"So remind me," said Billy, "what have we got so far?"

Charley pulled out her notebook and, licking the tip of her finger, she flipped through the pages. "Last year Sir Gordon funded an expedition led by…" She scanned her small neat writing, searching for the name. "Alan Quinn."

Billy rubbed his chin. "He's a bit of a lowlife from what I hear."

"You know him?"

"I know *of* him," said Billy. "I've got a cousin who runs a gambling den and I remember there was an Alan Quinn who played cards for high stakes and built up so much debt he had to leave the country. Last I heard he was out in Africa, organizing big-game hunting and safaris for wealthy nobility. Archaeology isn't his usual line at all."

"He did incredibly well for his first dig then," said Charley, "considering the vast haul they brought home. Did he just get lucky?"

"More likely Quinn was just hired muscle. You know how these things work – the rich man says where he wants to dig, and the poor men do the digging."

"Sir Gordon is the one with a passion for Egyptology, so I suppose it's possible that *he* was the one who worked out where to find the tomb. He certainly takes all the credit."

"He didn't seem like a 'mastermind' to me," said Billy.

"But if Sir Gordon didn't discover the tomb," said Charley, "then who did?"

"Probably one of the local Egyptians. Who would know where the treasure was buried better than them?"

"Who indeed?" said Charley, placing a big question mark at the foot of her page.

"So what about this rampaging mummy?" Billy leaned forward in his seat. "Any theories?"

Charley ticked them off. "It could be a hoax, someone trying to frighten Sir Gordon for some reason. An actor paid to play a gruesome role. Possibly Sir Gordon cheated Quinn out of his rightful share and this is his revenge."

"Possibly. Or?"

"It might be a genuine mummy, risen from its centuries-long sleep and fulfilling its curse."

Billy sat back, satisfied. "We've not done a mummy before."

"Don't get your hopes up," said Charley. "Remember that 'mermaid' we were called in to investigate?"

Billy nodded. "Where it turned out that the man who ran the Hall of Curiosities had sewn half a dead monkey to half a dead fish." He pulled a face. "Disgusting, wasn't it? And how about the werewolf woman of Hampstead Heath?"

"Or, as we came to call her, the unfortunately hairy old lady of Hampstead Heath."

They both laughed.

"But the imp was real, wasn't it?" said Billy. "Remember how it spat when we captured it."

"Six inches tall and teeth like a piranha."

"And what about that boggart?"

"Tough case," said Charley. "I never thought we'd get it back in its hole."

"But a real mummy," said Billy wistfully. "That would be something special."

"Fingers crossed," said Charley. "Let's open the file, see what else Luther has got for us."

Billy couldn't help but grin as he pulled out the scarlet file, sealed with wax. Normal police files were manila, boring old brown. Serious and gruesome crimes were in black folders. But S.C.R.E.A.M. files were red. Red for unknown, red for strange. Red for danger.

Billy cracked open the seal with his thumb, and excitedly leafed through the pages inside. "Lots of information on ancient Egypt…"

"Lovely light reading for the journey," said Charley.

"Hello?" said Billy, pulling a document from the pack. "Luther has included some information from the Edinburgh police – he must think that it's connected."

"Let me see," said Charley, scanning the page, eager to get to the juicy bits. "It's a burglary report. Police were called to the home of Lady Marigold Tiffin to investigate reports that her necklace, the famous Dalton diamonds, had been stolen. Blah, blah, blah…" She paused. "Luther has put a note in the margin – apparently Lady M was a guest at the mummy unwrapping."

"Coincidence?" said Billy.

"Doubt it," said Charley. "Luther Sparkwell believes in a lot of things, but coincidence isn't one of them." She read on. "There's a statement from a Mrs Whisker, housekeeper to the Tiffin family for nearly twenty years—"

"Let me guess," Billy interrupted. "She didn't see anything."

Charley shook her head. "Oh ye of little faith," she teased. "She actually said, 'I didn't see nuthin'.'"

"They never do," Billy sighed.

"Inspector Diggins, who's investigating the burglary, insists that he will 'dig out the truth'."

Billy sighed again, louder this time. "I bet he says that all the time."

"You'll like this though," said Charley. "Traces of *sand* were found at the crime scene, which suggests our mummy really was involved." Her face lit up. "Are you thinking what I'm thinking?"

"You'd kill for a bacon sandwich?"

Charley smiled. "I don't think this mummy is working alone."

"How do you make that out?"

"Imagine you are a five-thousand-year-old mummy, recently risen from the dead to walk the earth again… What could you possibly want with diamonds?"

"So if we find who wants the diamonds then we might find who is behind all this," said Billy excitedly.

"Exactly! And who wants diamonds?"

"Everybody in the world," said Billy. "Doesn't really narrow it down much, does it?"

The ten-and-a-half hour journey up the Great Northern Line grew into a miserable and tiring fifteen-hour journey. Engineering works on the track held up the train for what felt like an eternity, and a further delay at York turned a half-hour lunch stop into two more wasted hours. As the Special Scotch Express dragged itself the last two hundred miles to Waverley station in Edinburgh, Billy and Charley were both flagging, the rocking of the carriage lulling them into the waiting arms of sleep.

Billy didn't know how long he had been sleeping. The train compartment was chilly and the seat was so hard that Billy actually felt more tired *now* than he had done before he nodded off. His back ached, his mouth was dry and his eyes were crusty. Still half asleep, Billy poked his finger into the corner of his eye. "Sleepy dust", his mother called it. But this felt different, wrong somehow.

There was so much of it. Not just a few specks near his tear duct, but dozens and dozens right across his eye.

Billy rubbed more intently, feeling *hundreds* of grains; sharp and hard against his skin. He tried to open his eyes to blink the stuff away, but it felt as if his eyelids were glued shut. There were clumps of the foul grit gumming his eyelashes together, so much that he had to really strain before they pulled apart and he could see again. By now, Billy's heart was punching against his ribcage, like a boxer in the fight of his career.

His mouth was as dry as a desert. Billy poked out his tongue to moisten his lips and instantly regretted it. His lips were coated with grains too and now the inside of his mouth was full of the stuff. Billy coughed and spat while his hands frantically brushed his hair, his shoulders, chest, arms, legs. Everywhere.

Urgently Billy glanced over to where Charley was still sleeping. It looked as if frost had settled on her. She was covered from head to foot in tiny granules, the moonlight through the window making the crystals glisten coldly.

But it was not ice.

They had both been covered with sand.

Pushing down his rising sense of dread, Billy roused Charley gently.

"Charley," he said softly. "Don't be afraid, but something has happened to us."

32

She moaned, as all sleepers do when the joy of dreaming has to end too soon. But then she felt the sand clinging to every pore of her skin and she was instantly awake.

Charley shook her long ginger hair and sent a thousand grains spilling to the floor of the carriage. Calmly – *Much more calmly than me*, Billy thought – she flicked the sand from her clothes.

"It's a message," said Charley, pointing to a square of parchment on the floor.

With sand beneath his nails and in the corners of his mouth, Billy picked it up and read:

TURN BACK NOW.
YOU HAVE BEEN WARNED!
THE SANDMAN

CHAPTER THREE

SOMETHING IN THE DARKNESS

Billy dashed out into the corridor. His head snapped back and forth, searching the shadows for movement. His inner sixth sense was reaching out, searching the invisible realm for traces of the supernatural.

Something had been there, Billy knew. There was a taint in the air – an oily smokiness which only Billy could detect – and a metallic tang in his mouth like blood. Magick had passed this way, he was certain. Old and dangerous magick.

But the traces were faint and fading fast.

"We're too late," he told Charley with a snarl, as he

stumbled back into their carriage. Billy's "gift" came at a price; each time he used it he was left drained. Right now he could barely stand and was clinging to the door frame for support.

Billy breathed in through his nose, his head clearing as the scent grew cold. "'The Sandman' is long gone."

Charley shuddered. "It's monstrous to think that someone was in here, watching us while we slept."

Billy closed the compartment door again, although it didn't make him feel any safer. "Do you think Sir Gordon is being followed?" he wondered out loud, scratching his head and dislodging still more sand. The train shuddered then and began to slow. "Edinburgh, finally," declared Billy, looking through the window and seeing the unmistakable silhouette of the castle looming over the city.

"Quick," said Charley. "Gather up some of the sand in an envelope, I want to analyze it as soon as we get to our lodgings."

"Isn't sand just sand?"

Charley gave a theatrical sigh. "How simple it must be in your world, Billy Flint."

"Right," said Charley, as she steered her wicker wheelchair towards the open train door and the platform that lay beyond it. "This is how we're going to do it." She spotted a porter and waved him over. "He can take the weight on the footrest while you support me with the handles."

"You don't want me to just bump you down on my own then, like we do on stairs?"

"Only if you want to tip me out," said Charley. "Honestly, you can tell who's got the brains on this team."

Once Charley was safely down on the platform, Billy left her to it. Charley had very strict rules about her chair. Charlotte Steel decided where she wanted to go for herself; nobody pushed her around.

Billy gathered up their bags. Charley had five to his one, he noticed. Typical girl.

At the far end of the platform Sir Gordon and his entourage were whisked away into a waiting coach without so much as a second glance in their direction.

"We're fine, thanks," Billy called out sarcastically. "But it was kind of you to offer."

"Forget it," said Charley, "we've got the address for the hotel. We can make our own way there." A cold rain was blowing in from the east and her teeth started to rattle in her jaw.

Billy shivered as the damp night air wormed its way

beneath his coat. "Lead on, Duchess," he said with a smile.

They were heading towards the exit when a small boy called out to them. "Hey, wait up!" said the lad. He came pounding along the platform towards them, a Scottish terrier bouncing at his side. "Did ye see any policemen on the train?" asked the boy anxiously, while the dog ran round and round him, tangling him in its lead. "Sir Gordon sent me… The footman should've come but he's run away, so I'm s'posed to take them to their hotel…only I fell asleep when the train was so late." The young lad looked at them, his eyes pleading like a puppy's, bigger even than the terrier's. "I'll get a hiding if I've missed them. Charles Steel and William Flint. Have ye seen them?"

"We *are* them," said Charley, extending her hand. "I am Detective Constable *Charlotte* Steel and this is Detective Constable Billy Flint."

"Away with you!" said the Scottish lad in disbelief. "He's only a few years older than me and you're a poor wee cripple."

Billy winced. Charley wouldn't take that lying down.

"You can believe it or not," said Charley, spinning her chair so her back was to him. "Come on, Billy. I'm not in the mood for this."

37

"I was on the lookout for two *men*," the boy explained, dodging round to face her and whipping his cap from his head as a mark of respect. "I'm Doogie McCrimmon," he said, "and I'm sorry for my mistake, miss."

Charley pushed her chair forward until one wheel was crushing Doogie's foot. Doogie winced. Charley rocked the wheel slightly, until she heard him whimper. "All forgiven," she said breezily. "Who's your friend?"

"My...? Och," said Doogie, realizing she was talking about the dog. "This handsome laddie is Wellington."

"Pleased to meet you, Wellington," said Charley, rubbing his ears. Wellington gazed back at her from beneath formidable doggy eyebrows. He really was a fine animal, with a beautiful black coat. Pedigree undoubtedly.

"Lead on," said Charley.

Doogie hesitated, unsure whether she was talking to him or the dog, then he snatched up three of their bags and lumbered off, swaying under their weight. "This way," he said.

The weather was worsening by the moment, the drizzle turning into small hard pellets of rain. They followed Doogie with their heads down and their collars turned up.

"Welcome to Scotland," muttered Billy.

38

Suddenly Wellington tensed. The dog stood stock-still, fur bristling, a growl vibrating in his throat.

"Come on now," urged Doogie, straining under the weight of the bags.

"Wait," said Billy.

"What is it?" asked Charley.

"I'm not sure," said Billy, sticking out his tongue. "But it tastes evil."

They were all alert now, eyes trying to pierce the darkness, searching for the danger that Billy and Wellington could sense.

"There!" snapped Billy, pointing into the shadows. At that instant Wellington broke free from his lead and the pair of them sprinted away. Charley was half a second behind. For a fleeting instant she thought she could see a silhouette, lurking in an archway. The figure had the body of a man and the head of a...what was it? A crocodile!

Its cover blown, the hulking shape retreated. "Stop in the name of the law!" Charley shouted. Doogie whipped a small knife from out of his sock and brandished it as he ran alongside her.

Panting, Billy reached the spot where they'd seen the figure hiding. But he was too late. Whoever – *whatever* –

it was, had gone. How long had it been there? What did it want?

Wellington was barking ferociously at the empty air. Bizarrely, there was a whirlwind of sand twirling on the floor and it was driving the small dog crazy. Billy watched the vortex. Ordinary people might have dismissed it as the wind eddying, but Billy could taste the lingering tang of magick all around. It was the same oily mixture of blood and smoke that he had sensed on the train. The Sandman again?

Charley and Doogie arrived in time to see the last grains of sand spin to a slow halt. The final traces of magick faded away too. Charley raised her eyebrow. "What a curious phenomenon."

"Did ye see it?" gasped Doogie. "Did ye see the beastie?" He still held his knife, his *dirk*, but his hand was visibly shaking. "I think we must have scared it off."

"I doubt that," said Billy.

"But how did it get away from us? It must have been at least six foot tall," said Charley. "It can't have just disappeared."

"Stranger things have happened," said Billy.

"Yes," said Charley, "especially to us."

CHAPTER FOUR

RAG-AND-BONE MAN

The coach that Sir Gordon had sent to take them to the hotel looked fit for a king. The body was painted dark green, with Sir Gordon's family crest on the door. The wheels were red. Billy didn't see any of that though, he only saw the four creatures that were pulling it. They looked like horses, only smaller. Small horses with black and white stripes.

"What the...?" Billy began.

"Zebras," said Charley. "Natives of the African grasslands."

"They must feel right at home here then," said Billy,

41

hugging himself against the chill.

Doogie stroked one of the zebras on the muzzle. "His Lordship has his special ways," he said. "Ye get used to it. Sort of."

They made the journey to the hotel in silence. Despite its luxurious appearance, the carriage was uncomfortable. The leather seats were hard and it was bitterly cold even with blankets to cover their legs. Somewhere a piper was playing and the sound floated through the night air. The tune was haunting and strangely beautiful at the same time; somehow it fitted their mood precisely.

"Here we are," said Doogie eventually, as the zebras whinnied and the carriage juddered to a halt. Billy and Charley looked out of the window to see a tall foreboding building. The moon had helpfully positioned itself behind the turreted roof to make sure that it looked truly sinister. A pair of stone gargoyles stood guard on the gateposts, rain dripping from their gaping mouths and savage claws. Everything about it said *Run away*, rather than *Come on in and put your feet up*.

"I love what they've done with the place," said Charley. "Creepy *and* unwelcoming. I'm amazed more hotels don't go for that."

Billy shuddered and turned up the collar on his coat

before stepping out. "Best make the most of it, eh?"

Doing their best to ignore the rain, Billy and the driver helped Charley down from the carriage between them, while Doogie untied the wheelchair from the luggage rack on the back so that it was waiting for her on the pavement. Charley quickly got comfortable while Billy was busy removing the rest of their luggage from the roof. Wellington wisely stayed inside.

When they were ready, the driver clicked his tongue to the shivering zebras and flicked the reins. Doogie waved goodbye from the window. "We'll be back to collect ye in the morning."

Billy and Charley approached the front door and knocked. After what felt like an age they heard jangling keys and footsteps approaching on the other side of the door. Without much of a welcome they were beckoned inside by a tiny old woman, whose eyes, skin, hair and dressing gown all seemed to be the same washed-out grey. They followed her down a dingy corridor until she brought them to a halt outside two neighbouring doors. "Here are your keys. Two singles, both on the ground floor as requested. I can see why now," she said with a pointed look at Charley. "Such a shame for a pretty lass too."

"It would be so much better if I was ugly, wouldn't it?" said Charley.

The landlady bristled. "I'm sure you'll have had your tea," she said shortly. "So if that's all, I'll bid you goodnight and retire to my own bed."

It wasn't all, as far as Billy's stomach was concerned. He wanted a baked potato, or some soup, or some bread and cheese at least. Charley wanted a nice cup of tea, Early Grey preferably, or Assam at a push. But as soon as their doors were unlocked, the old lady was up the stairs and away.

"Come into my room for a while," said Charley. "I've got a couple of sandwiches left, I'm sure."

Billy was soon wolfing down the remains of Charley's packed lunch. "What are you having?"

"Brain food, dear Billy," she replied, unpacking her microscope and setting it up on the dressing table. She slipped off her watch pendant, placing it carefully to one side, then she rolled up her sleeves ready to work. "Do you have the sand samples we collected?"

"One from the train carriage and one from the station." Billy fished two envelopes out of his pocket. "But I still don't know what you can find out from this."

"Watch and learn," said Charley, sprinkling a few of

44

the grains onto a slide and examining them through the magnifying lens.

"Aaaah," said Charley after a few moments. "Mmmm."

"Let me in then, Duchess," said Billy. "Sounds like you're having too much fun without me."

"Well…" began Charley, and Billy settled back in an armchair. She was using her "lecture" voice – they could be here a while. "You know how the sand is different on different beaches, sometimes white, other times gold or grey or even black—"

"Do the banks of the Thames count as a beach?"

"Much sand down there?" asked Charley.

"Nahhh," said Billy. "Just loads of…" He paused, searching for the right word, found it, then decided that he couldn't say it in front of a lady. "Loads of *mud*," he said eventually. "Stinking piles of it."

"I get the picture," said Charley. "So you've never been to an actual beach?"

Billy shrugged. "Seaside holidays aren't big in the Flint family. Breaking and entering however…barrel of laughs."

Charley pulled a face. The criminal behaviour of the rest of Billy's enormous family was a subject they normally kept clear of. "Anyway," she said, "believe me when I tell you that sand comes in a variety of colours depending on the minerals, rocks and other materials which make it up."

"Different colours, different rocks," said Billy. "So?"

"So there are *thousands* of different types of sand. Biogenic sand contains the skeletal remains of coral, barnacles and gastropod molluscs. There is blue sand in Namibia, star garnet sand in Idaho. No two deserts, no two beaches, no two riverbeds have exactly the same combination. Every grain of sand tells a story…"

"So what is this sand telling us?"

Charley smiled. Billy smiled too; she had good news.

"This sand, Billy, has come a very long way…from the Sahara Desert, in fact."

"Where the mummies are," said Billy.

"Exactly." Charley was triumphant.

"How do you know all this anyway?"

She reached over and patted his cheek. "They hide information in books."

Billy was still trying to think of a witty comeback – something along the lines of "Blow it out your backside" – when a shrill yell pierced the night.

"*Help me!*"

46

It was a woman's voice, screaming, and it was followed by the unmistakable sound of slapping feet running full pelt over the cobbles outside. Whoever she was, she was running for her life.

"Save yourselves… It's a monster!"

"That sounds like our cue!" said Billy. The pair of them were at the window in a flash, throwing back the curtain and peering into the rainswept gloom. The terrified woman was nowhere in sight but a solitary figure stood in the middle of the street, illuminated by the flickering gas lamps. A figure wrapped from head to foot in filthy bandages, arms outstretched.

Spotting the light in their window, the mummy turned towards them and lurched in their direction. Billy closed the curtains again. Too late. They'd been seen.

"Quick!" he said. "The door."

Charley manoeuvred her chair within the confines of the small room, heading for the only way out. Her hand was on the doorknob when the window shattered.

A fist burst through the glass, and they both watched as rag-covered fingers grabbed the curtains and yanked them down, ripping one end of the curtain rail from the wall. The mummy stood outside, reaching in, fingers now grasping at thin air.

47

The stench of putrid flesh filled the room and a strangled moan escaped from its ancient lips.

"*Uuuuuuurrrrrrrggggggggggghhhhhhhhhhhhhhhhhh!*"

The mummy punched more of the splintered windowpane out of the way.

Billy staggered backwards, throwing up his arms to shield his face from the shards of broken glass flying towards him like tiny daggers. He felt a sharp sting on his forehead, followed by a hot trickle of blood rolling over one eyebrow. *If that had been an inch lower…*

Blinking away the blood, Billy saw that the creature was still desperately trying to break in. Its head and shoulders were through the shattered window and both hands were grasping, sharp finger bones exposed. For a frozen second, Billy couldn't drag his gaze away from those terrible hands.

It was a second too long.

With frightening speed, the skeletal hand grasped Billy's arm.

"No!" Charley shouted, but even as Billy heard her warning, he felt his head begin to swim.

His gift allowed him to sense magick, the supernatural, the unnatural – all those intangible powers, those invisible forces could briefly become clear to him, as if a curtain existed between two rooms and for a moment it was drawn aside, allowing Billy a glimpse of what lay beyond…whether he liked it or not.

But up this close, actually in the grips of a five-thousand-year-old creature that should have stayed dead and buried, Billy's sixth sense was overwhelmed.

The grave stink of the mummy washed over Billy as image after image struck his mind, like the blows of a hammer…

The pyramids. The stillness of the tomb. The cold of the coffin. The darkness. The silence. The eternity of death… Then the light as the stone lid of the sarcophagus was lifted… Immortal sleep disturbed. The taste of wax in his mouth. The pain! The anger! Ancient gods with monstrous faces, towering above him… A crocodile, massive jaws waiting to snap… A lioness, her mouth a silent roar. A jackal, lips drawn back in a snarl… And another figure…a shaven-headed figure… a powerful man…a man of cunning and magick—

BANG!

The sound of the gun being fired was enough to snap Billy out of his trancelike state. He saw Charley holding her pistol calmly in both hands, blue smoke coiling from the barrel. Billy felt the cold grip of the mummy's hands on his arms, tighter than vices. With a snarl, the mummy shook Billy from side to side as if he was a rag doll.

Charley's lip curled back in frustration. Her finger paused on the trigger; she couldn't risk shooting Billy. "Just stay still, damn it!"

Billy did his best to resist the creature, but in spite of the fact that its muscles had long since shrivelled away to nothing, there was still incredible strength in those arms. Little by little, Billy was being dragged towards the jagged mouth of the broken window.

A second bullet sang out and Billy saw it hit the mummy square in the shoulder. The force of the impact rocked the creature back on its heels, but there was no sign that it had actually been wounded except for a trickle of sand which bled from the smoking hole left in the bandages.

Billy was struggling with all his might now, twisting and turning as he tried to wrench free of the mummy's cold grip, but he was losing and he knew it. Charley positioned herself for another shot, this time aiming for the head. It was another direct hit, of course, and it knocked the mummy's head back on its neck a full ninety degrees.

The mummy's head hung there for a moment, as if it was only the bandages that stopped it from falling off and rolling down the street. But then, impossibly, the head began to rise again and Billy winced as the skeletal grip tightened around his arms.

"It's no good," Billy breathed. "You get out of here, Charley."

"Shut up trying to be brave and let me solve this, will you?"

There was a small table by the bed with an oil lamp sitting on it. Billy saw Charley look at it, a small smile lighting up the corners of her mouth.

She quickly crossed the room and picked up the lighted lamp.

"No, Charley," said Billy. "It's too risky." He thrashed around in desperation, doing everything that he could to break the mummy's hold on him.

"You'll need to get out of the way really quickly then," said Charley, raising the lamp.

Billy knew that she meant it. In a last-ditch effort, he lifted both of his feet off the floor, planted them firmly on the window sill and launched himself back with all his might. His jacket sleeves ripped off and were left dangling in the skeletal fingers, but Billy was free! Gasping with relief he fell onto the bed just as Charley's missile soared through the air above him.

Once again, the mummy responded with terrifying speed. The oil lamp would have struck it square on the chest, but with one sweep of its arm the creature batted it out of the way to smash against the bedroom wall. Instantly the burning oil took hold. Dozens of flaming drops splashed in every direction, and the moth-eaten bedspread, the stained wallpaper and the threadbare rug all flared into life.

The mummy did not escape unscathed. The arm which had deflected the firebomb was drenched in oil. Charley might have been mistaken, but she could have sworn that there was a note of panic in the creature's voice as the first flame took hold.

"*Aarrrrrrrrrrrrrrrggggggggghhhhhhhhhhh!*" the mummy wailed as the fire spread up its bandaged arm. It flailed around as it tried to manoeuvre itself back out of the window, setting the curtains on fire before finally falling backwards out into the rain-drenched night.

Inside the room the fire had taken hold of the broken curtain rail and was starting to attack the ceiling. Charley grasped Billy's hand and dragged him towards the door. Billy didn't resist. Charley only paused to snatch up her microscope and dump it on her lap.

"Quick!" said Billy, "before the whole place goes up!"

52

CHAPTER FIVE

THE TEMPLE OF THE SEVEN STARS

The Temple of the Seven Stars was cold and dark and oh-so-secret. Down here, in his underground lair, the Sandman ruled. He sat on his golden throne, his hand stroking the smooth dome of his bald head, while he dreamed his favourite dream; a dream of cold bright diamonds and steaming hot revenge. Tall sandstone pillars supported the high ceiling that arched above him. The stonework had been painted a fierce midnight blue, swirling into deepest black, and was pierced with a thousand points of glistening white. It gave the impression that he wasn't in an underground tomb at all, but was sitting beneath the vastness of the night sky.

The stone floor was covered with carvings in the language of ancient Egypt. The hieroglyphic pictures and symbols declared that this was more than just a tomb; it was a portal between the Land of the Living and the Land of the Dead.

The Sandman was not alone. A king needed servants, after all. On a gold chain around his neck hung a pendant in the shape of a triangle surrounding a solitary lidless eye. The Eye of Horus belonged to him. *He* had the power and so *he* was the one who sat; the gods of Egypt could stand. The Sandman regarded them coolly.

Sobek the crocodile; savage and strong. The god of the Nile. Lord of soldiers. He who loved robbery. He of pointed teeth and insatiable hunger.

Sekhmet the lioness; sleek and deadly. The goddess of fire, war and vengeance. Mistress of the dead. Lady of slaughter. She who mauls.

Anubis the jackal; proud and powerful. The god of funerals and death. The protector of the grave. Master of mummification.

The Sandman smiled. All he had to do was click his fingers… But for now he had to wait. Waiting came easily to him; it was what he did, day in, day out. But the waiting had never felt like this before.

Good things come to those who wait. Wasn't that what people said?

The Sandman chuckled; an angry snort, brimming with bitterness. *And bad things come to those who oppose me!*

"You were meant to scare away those meddling investigators at the station!" he snarled.

Sobek the crocodile sank his massive head, admitting his failure. "I was disturbed."

The Sandman glowered. "I will not accept failure a second time."

Sobek said nothing.

On the floor in front of the golden throne there was a circle of fine sand. Using the tip of a curved bone, the Sandman drew a series of hieroglyphs, powerful symbols that together made a magical incantation. Pleased with his work, the Sandman watched and the sand began to stir…

First one lonely grain began a slow circuit, impossibly bouncing round and round. Then another grain started to move, then another, and another. Spinning faster and faster until the entire circle was whirling in a blur and rising into the air like a tornado of sand.

And something was materializing inside it.

"He returns!" the Sandman declared triumphantly as the mummy appeared inside the magical sandstorm.

"UuuuuuuuuuuuuuuuuUUUUUUUUUHHHHHHH," it growled, like an animal in pain. Suddenly the sand dropped to the ground, the magick done, and the mummy stood there, arms outstretched.

The Sandman held his breath as the mummy stumbled towards him. Although it was under his control it had lost none of its power to terrify him. Beneath the filthy grave wrappings was the body and skeleton of a man. The embalming wax – the *mūm*, which gave all mummies their name – had done its job well. Chunks of leathery flesh had been preserved and still hung on the frame of bones.

The stench was even worse than before. Mixed with the reek of decay was the sweet tang of cooked meat and the harsh sooty smell that lingers after a fire.

"What have they done to you, my beauty?" said the Sandman, shocked to see that one of the mummy's arms had lost almost all of its bandages and been burned down to gristle and bone.

"I have more wax," the Sandman said in a comforting tone, like a mother to a child, "and more bandages. You'd like that, wouldn't you?"

The mummy nodded, another gurgle spilling from its leathery lips.

"I need you fighting fit," said the Sandman. "We've only just begun… Vengeance shall be mine!" He threw back his head and laughed and laughed. The sound echoed through the Temple of the Seven Stars.

The gods of Egypt trembled.

CHAPTER SIX

THE SCENE OF THE CRIME

A ghostly sun rose in the bone-white Edinburgh sky. The streets were just beginning to stir as a zebra-drawn carriage clattered over the cobbles, drawing to a halt outside the blackened wreckage of the hotel.

"Jings!" Doogie McCrimmon declared, his mouth as wide as a saucer. "And I thought *I* had news."

"The mummy attacked us," said Billy, sitting on his suitcase, which he'd rescued from the flames. "Oh, and the hotel burned down." Billy smiled, but the dark lines under his eyes showed how long the night had been.

"Not much sleep then," said Doogie.

"We'll survive," said Billy.

Doogie climbed down from the carriage and stood in front of the smouldering remains, the zebras snorting and stamping as they breathed in the smoky air. Spotting Charley, Doogie whipped off his cap. "Are ye all right, Miss Steel?"

"It takes more than an assassination attempt and a raging inferno to upset me. Now," she said with a smile, "you said something about 'news'?"

"There's been another burglary," said Doogie, "and the mummy was there."

Charley clapped gleefully. "Oh, that *is* good news."

"Really?" said Doogie. "When is a burglary good news?"

"When you're a detective, my dear Doogie," said Charley, patting his arm. "A new burglary gives me and my partner a fresh crime scene to investigate."

"Do ye not want to visit Sir Gordon's house now, miss?" said Doogie, looking at their bedraggled clothes and soot-smeared faces. "Maybes freshen up a bit first?"

"Certainly not," said Charley. "We mustn't let the trail go cold!"

Inside the carriage, their luggage safely stowed on the roof, Charley took a small mirror from her bag. She examined her reflection, then wiped her face clean with a fresh handkerchief and ran a brush through her luxurious red hair until it shone like polished bronze.

"How do I look?" she asked.

"Fit for the palace, same as always," said Billy. He licked the palm of his hand, rubbed it roughly over his face, then licked it again and tried to smooth down a spike of hair that was sticking up from his head like a horn. As an afterthought he lifted his arm and gave a sniff. He grimaced. "How about me?"

"Fit for the workhouse," Charley answered with a smile.

"I'm improving then," said Billy. "The last time you said I was only fit for the gutter."

"I was being kind," said Charley.

"Where to?" called the driver.

"Let the dog see the rabbit," said Billy.

The carriage didn't move.

"He means, 'Please take us to the next crime scene, my good man,'" Charley explained. "And be quick about it."

The zebras whinnied and they were off, rattling through the streets until they came to a halt outside an impressive three-storey house built from Edinburgh's famous red granite. Billy whistled softly between his teeth. "Nice gaff," he said admiringly as he and Doogie helped Charley out of the carriage and into her wheelchair. "Who lives here?"

"Lady Lavinia Fitzpatrick," said Doogie. "A friend of Sir Gordon."

Billy nodded. "Makes sense. And was she at the mummy unwrapping party?"

"Aye," said Doogie.

"Can you tell us anything about Lady Fitzpatrick?" said Charley, her eyes glistening at the thrill of the chase.

Doogie scratched his head and then his face lit up. "Och yes," he said. "She's got a bahookie as big as a horse." He bent over slightly and slapped his own backside, just for emphasis.

"Yes," said Charley. "Thank you." Then quickly added, "Why don't you wait in the carriage?" Doogie's face dropped. Charley felt as if she had just kicked a particularly cute puppy.

"Sorry," said Billy, patting Doogie on the arm to show no hard feelings. "This is police business."

Billy and Charley approached the front door just as a constable was leaving. Charley gave the bobby her brightest smile. Billy flicked him a salute. The constable did not seem pleased to see them. Even his moustache looked annoyed.

"Move along," said the policeman curtly, making a sweeping movement with his gloved hand. "Nothing to see here."

"On the contrary," said Charley, "there's a great deal to see." She flicked open her warrant card with a flourish. "So be a good chap and show us in, will you?"

The constable looked at Billy and Charley and the silly smiles on their faces. He examined their badges. "Is this some kind of joke?"

"Only if you find the living dead amusing," said Billy.

"What are you talking about?" he blustered.

"We're experts from London," said Charley. "We know more than you can begin to imagine."

"Have it your way," said the constable, with scowl. "If the Metropolitan Police Force wants to use children to do a man's job, that's up to them." He stood aside to let them pass. "It's a madhouse in there." He bent low and whispered angrily, "You're on your own."

"That's just the way we like it," said Charley.

CHAPTER SEVEN

IT'S ALL ABOUT THE MUMMY

The constable was right about one thing. The grand house was in a state of hysteria. Sobbing could be heard coming from behind the closed door of the drawing room. A young maid sat at the foot of the sweeping staircase, her head in her hands. The poor girl was crying too, mumbling to herself between her tears. "Risen from the grave," she muttered. "The stench! The power of those dead arms! And an awful mess in the study…I'll be all day clearing that." She started to cry again.

A man in a butler's uniform spotted Billy and Charley hovering in the hallway. "Out!" he shouted. "Her

Ladyship will not be seeing any visitors today!"

"She'll see us, mate," said Billy, flashing his police badge. "Billy Flint and Charlotte Steel, S.C.R.E.A.M. squad."

Even though he was wearing white gloves, the butler took Billy's open wallet with his forefinger and thumb, as if it was something that the cat had dragged in. He studied it carefully, his head swaying slightly as his glance went from Billy to Charley and back again. It was almost hypnotic, Charley thought; the butler reminded her of a snake or a lizard. There was definitely something cold-blooded about this man.

"And you are?" said Charley.

"I am Harris," the butler replied. He handed Billy's wallet back, then paused to wipe his gloved hands on his trouser leg. "The *official* police have just left," he said. "We've already told Inspector Diggins everything we know. Why do you insist on distressing Her Ladyship even further?"

"We've not come to upset anyone," said Billy. "But you know as well as we do that this ain't no ordinary case."

"I don't know what you're talking about," said Harris.

Billy raised his arms in front of him and lumbered

around the hall going, *"Uuuurrrrrrgggggggghhhhhhhh…*
Does that ring any bells, mate?"

"Inspector Diggins is convinced that the bandages are some sort of disguise."

"Daft sort of disguise if you ask me. Is he very bright, this Inspector Diggins?"

"What my colleague is trying to say is that Detective Constable Flint and myself are London experts in…how shall we put it? *Peculiar* crimes. No one on the force is better placed to help Her Ladyship than us."

Harris hesitated. "Forgive me," he said. "This has been a trying time for all of us… My first thought, *as always*, is for Her Ladyship's wellbeing."

"Haaaa-rris!" A loud voice rang out and Harris hurried away obediently.

The butler returned a minute later. "Her Ladyship has generously agreed that she will meet with *you* in private, Miss Steel." Harris turned and looked daggers at Billy. "You can wait downstairs in the servants' quarters."

"Suits me," said Billy. "I know my place." He made a show of wiping his nose on his sleeve. Harris pulled a disapproving face. "Plus," Billy continued with a grin, "I've got some questions of my own that need answering. Like where was everyone at the time of the crime, and when can I get a bacon sandwich? I'm starving."

Charley smiled privately as she watched Harris lead Billy away. She knew full well that Billy's cheeky urchin routine was just that – an act, intended to keep his suspects off guard.

Charley found the lady of the house pacing backwards and forwards in her drawing room. The woman was every bit as fat as Doogie had described but, unlike Sir Gordon, there was strength in every line of her face. Even so, it looked to Charley as if Lady Fitzpatrick had seen the most terrible thing in the world. She could almost taste the woman's fear.

"I'm Detective Constable Charlotte Steel, S.C.R.E.A.M. squad, Metropolitan Police," Charley introduced herself. "I'm pleased to meet you, Lady Fitzpatrick."

Lady Fitzpatrick turned to face her. "Charlotte *Steel*… Not related to Sir Simon Steel, by any chance?"

"He's my father."

"Oh," said Lady Fitzpatrick, confused and embarrassed. "But Sir Simon told me that his daughter was at a finishing school in Switzerland." The old woman tried to look anywhere except at Charley's wheelchair.

"It was a sanatorium actually," said Charley, "for my

health. But it was so very dull that I couldn't stand it. So now I'm back in Britain solving supernatural crimes for a living."

"Oh," said Lady Fitzpatrick again, lost for words.

"Polio, if you were wondering." Charley leaned forwards, as if to share a secret. "Just between you and me," she said, "I don't know which annoys my father more – that I'm stuck in this wretched chair, or that, rather than sitting around waiting for someone to marry me, I've got myself a job instead." She smiled. "On that note, I'd very much like to see the crime scene."

"Let me show you now," said Lady Fitzpatrick. "And then I think I will never set foot in that room again. Except in my nightmares."

CHAPTER EIGHT

WRITTEN IN THE SAND

"I was sitting there," Lady Fitzpatrick explained, pointing to an armchair beside the fire. "I'm a bit of a night owl so I'm often reading late into the night. It was Daddy's favourite room too." She sighed. "He was a lovely man...such a beautiful moustache."

Charley felt at home with the oak-panelled walls, impressive bookcase and the delightful watercolour paintings of Highland scenes. But right now she wasn't interested in any of those things; she was a detective, and she was looking for clues. "Start at the beginning and tell me everything."

68

"I heard a scream and then some china breaking," said Lady Fitzpatrick. "My first thought was that it was my new maid. She's got a good heart but butterfingers. Costing me a fortune in teacups... Anyway, the disturbance grew louder and I realized that it had to be something more."

"Why?"

"The screaming didn't stop, for one thing. And then there were the footsteps." Lady Fitzpatrick shuddered. "The whole floor shook... To my shame I was frozen to the spot – I couldn't do anything except grip the arms of my chair as the footsteps came closer and closer."

"And what about Harris, your butler? Didn't he come to see what the disturbance was?"

"It was his night off unfortunately," Lady Fitzpatrick went on. "And anyway, I don't think that anyone would have been able to stop that...*thing*. Before I could even call for help, the creature burst in through the door. I know that I won't forget that moment until my dying day..."

Charley placed her hand gently on Lady Fitzpatrick's arm. "I know it's difficult, but whatever you can tell me might help to stop this from happening to someone else."

Lady Fitzpatrick took a deep breath. "The smell hit

me first…the rotting sweetness of meat that has been left in the sun." She shuddered at the memory. "Then I saw it… The grinning teeth and yellowed bones showing through the filthy grave clothes. One hand was charred, as if it had been burned –" she paused, questioning her own recollection of what she had seen – "but the bandages were white, not black. Strange. But who said that nightmares have to make sense? It was all so…*terrible.*

"I thought that it had come for me and I backed away against the wall. I even grabbed a poker from the fire to defend myself with."

Charley gave an approving smile.

"Fortunately, it ignored me completely, thank the Lord," Lady Fitzpatrick continued. "Instead it went straight over to my safe, hidden behind the portrait of my father…"

Charley saw the painting propped against the wall; the man really *did* have a glorious moustache.

Coolly and calmly, Charley pulled out her magnifying glass and began her examination. There were traces of sand on the carpet and she collected a few grains, storing them in a test tube. Then she focused her attention on the safe. The door had been ripped from its hinges… She turned to Lady Fitzpatrick. "How did it do this?"

"With its bare hands," said Lady Fitzpatrick.

Charley tried to take it in, her brain racing as she calculated how much physical strength it would take to do that sort of damage. The safe door had been torn clean off, the metal hinges shorn in two by the mummy's bare hands. She gasped – she couldn't help it. *Those same hands had grabbed Billy…it could have been him in two pieces.*

"So tell me what happened," said Billy, sitting opposite the maid. "From the beginning."

The girl had dried her tears now, but she was very young and it wouldn't take much to set her off again. "I don't know what went on upstairs. I'm only allowed in Her Ladyship's rooms if I'm cleaning them, but I can show you where the monster got in," she said. "The scullery."

"You've got a room to keep skulls in?"

"Don't be daft," she said, "the scullery is where we do all the laundry and washing-up. Come on, I'll show you."

Billy followed silently. He knew full well what a scullery was; he was just playing the fool to help put the frightened maid at ease.

"Why do you think the creature came from here?" he asked as they came around the corner. Then he saw the trail of sandy footprints, leading back to a circle of sand on the scullery floor. Billy dropped to his knees to investigate. First there was that swirling vortex of sand at the railway station, and now this. What could it mean? There were pictures in the sand too, although some of them had clearly been swept away, either by accident or on purpose. Billy took out his notebook and pencil and began to make a sketch of the remaining images. *A man; some strange fat animal's head; what might be a staff or magick wand.*

"And what about the doors?" Billy asked.

"All locked from the inside."

"And the windows? Any broken glass? Any sign that they might have been forced from the outside."

The maid shook her head. "The windows were all shut, Her Ladyship is most particular about it."

Billy picked up some of the sand and let it fall through his fingers. "I wonder," he said. "I wonder."

"So what was stolen?" asked Doogie as they rode away together in the zebra-drawn carriage, leaving Lady

Fitzpatrick and her troubled household behind.

"All of Her Ladyship's most treasured possessions," said Charley, reading a long and detailed list. "One sapphire and diamond ring; three cameo brooches; a pearl necklace; diamond earrings; a blue carbuncle pendant; pearl earrings; a rare bird's-claw kilt pin in eighteen-carat gold." She turned the page. "It goes on and on."

"Inspector Diggins can worry about getting the jewels back, we're only after the mummy," said Billy.

"On that subject, I found a strand of fibre snagged on the safe and it looked surprisingly clean for something which was meant to be thousands of years old."

Billy nodded, taking it in. "The servants confirmed Lady F's story," he said. "The mummy made straight for the secret safe. If it weren't for the fact that the burglar was thousands of years old and as dead as a doornail, I'd say this was a simple inside job."

Doogie nodded enthusiastically. "Servants are always pinching stuff from their employers."

Charley raised an eyebrow.

"Or so I'm told, anyhow," Doogie said quietly.

"No sign of forced entry, all the windows and doors were locked," said Billy, opening his notebook. "But what do you make of this?"

Charley examined the pictures eagerly. "Hieroglyphics," she said. "Ancient Egyptian picture language."

"Like a code," said Billy.

"Exactly," said Charley, "so I'd better get cracking. I've got some books in my luggage which might help. Translating ancient languages is never an easy task, and hieroglyphics are famously difficult to decipher."

"Each picture is a word," said Billy, showing the full extent of his knowledge.

"I wish it was that simple," said Charley, "but there's more to it than that, unfortunately. Not all pictures are words, some are sounds."

"Like letters."

"Yes, but some sounds that we use in English weren't used by the Egyptians at all, like 'th' – 'Thoth' may have been pronounced 'tote', for example. Whilst other sounds that we think are different, the Egyptians thought were the same, such as 'f' and 'v'. Anyway, that's when it starts to get *really* complicated." Charley knew that she was showing off a little, but she couldn't resist it.

"Most Egyptian scribes left out vowel sounds altogether and just used consonants. So to give the reader a clue as to the word they were writing they'd use an extra glyph, a determinative, on the end. Then there are ideograms – those are glyphs which represent a thing or an object without spelling it out. Plus, and this is the best bit, the hieroglyphs can be written left to right, right to left, vertically or horizontally."

Charley stopped in mid-flow and frowned at the paper Billy had given her. "What have you drawn here, Billy? Is that meant to be a dog?"

"It's a man," said Billy.

"Oh dear," Charley sighed. "This may take longer than I thought."

CHAPTER NINE

WALK LIKE AN EGYPTIAN

Sir Gordon's house was massive. More like a castle really, Billy thought, with its turrets and crenellated walls. A harassed-looking butler approached the carriage.

"I am Mr Cowley," he said. "This way if you please." He helped Charley down and then directed them inside with a small bow. "Sir Gordon is expecting you."

With a little help, Charley was able to get her wheelchair up the front step and the two detectives found themselves in a huge hallway, a shimmering chandelier above their heads. "Doogie will look after your luggage," said Cowley, "and rooms have been prepared for you upstairs."

Charley groaned inwardly as she took in the mountain of stairs that she would need to negotiate.

"We have a lift," Cowley added, as if reading her thoughts. "Sir Gordon had it installed last year at great expense. He is very proud that his house is the only private dwelling outside of London to have such a modern facility. We all so enjoy His Lordship's little... eccentricities." In a nervous gesture, Cowley's fingers briefly touched his perfect fringe, checking that not a single hair was out of place.

Billy and Charley followed silently, their heads turning left and right as they tried to take in their extraordinary surroundings. Many fashionable houses contained a "cabinet of curiosity", a collection of strange and wonderful objects from around the globe. Sir Gordon seemed to have turned his entire house into one enormous curiosity cabinet. The walls were crowded with exhibits and oddities. In frames. In display cases. Everywhere they turned they were surrounded by the macabre and the bizarre. Fierce masks from Africa. Bronze statues. Bones and skulls and beetles of every size and shape. Knives and axes and arrowheads from a hundred different tribes. A stuffed walrus suspended from the ceiling.

For Billy, it felt as if he was being assaulted on every side. Most houses had some supernatural traces in them. Faint footsteps of long-dead ghosts. The echoes of joy and sorrow lingering in the brickwork. Whispers from the spirit realm. But Sir Gordon's house was shouting at him. There was something very wrong in 44 Morningside Place.

Cowley opened the sliding doors of what appeared to be a metal cage and gestured for Billy and Charley to move into the small dark cave beyond. The butler stepped inside with them and then closed the doors with an ominous clang. The lift floor shuddered and, with a creak and groan of pulleys, it began to slowly rise, just as their spirits fell. They both felt it, not just Billy with his sixth sense. Some buildings can be rotted by damp; the joists and the floorboards – the bones of the house – silently decaying until the whole thing collapses. 44 Morningside Place was being eaten away by something darker and far more deadly.

Billy leaned in towards Charley and whispered, "What have we got ourselves into this time, Duchess?"

"And this is His Lordship's Egyptian hall," said Cowley, as they completed the grand tour of 44 Morningside Place. The butler opened the door for them but Billy placed a warning hand on Charley's shoulder.

"What is it?" asked Charley.

"Echoes of the tomb," said Billy softly.

Although she didn't have her partner's "gift", Charley understood – he was sensing something dangerous. She paused…and then went straight in. That was what S.C.R.E.A.M. detectives did.

Cowley had explained that some items had been destroyed when the mummy went on its rampage but there was still cabinet after cabinet full of Egyptian treasures. Pottery and jewellery and fragments of the past. Racks of gleaming weapons, statues of strange gods and beautiful women. And gold. So much gold. It was breathtaking. But what really held Charley's attention were the dead things.

Wrapped in rotting bandages they were assembled at the far end of the hall, like the strangest family that ever lived. Or died. From their outlines Charley could recognize the preserved remains of a cat, a monkey and a baby crocodile. Behind this disturbing gathering stood an upright coffin. Its door was open and its occupant was gone.

Beside her, Billy took a shuddering breath, but kept his thoughts to himself.

"Billy," she said, turning. But Billy wasn't there any more.

He was moving like a sleepwalker towards the open casket, heavy-footed and clumsy. His legs were stiff, as if he was suffering from *rigor mortis*, Charley recognized with horror; the rigidity that came over a corpse when the life had drained away.

"Billy," she said, louder this time, following him. If Billy heard her then he didn't show it. Charley spun her wheels and drew level with him. Billy was panting in short, sharp bursts. And this close she could see the trembling in his fingertips. His eyes were impossibly wide, the pupils expanded into deep dark holes, seeing only the sarcophagus – or perhaps into the spirit world beyond.

Cowley caught up with them. "Are ye all right, Master Flint?" he said.

Charley shushed him urgently. "I've seen him like this before," she said. "We mustn't wake him from the trance."

Billy's expression grew more intense. Now his eyes rolled up into his head until only the whites were showing and his eyelids fluttered rapidly. Charley hated to see Billy like this; whatever was happening to her friend, it looked like torture. And still Billy's focus remained on the empty sarcophagus...the last earthly resting place of the marauding mummy.

Billy continued to stumble forwards. Then suddenly, after half a dozen faltering paces, he picked up speed until he was half running, half falling towards that terrible open coffin.

Billy reached the sarcophagus. He stepped inside and turned around to face them, his eyes screwed tightly shut. Long seconds passed while he stood where the dead Egyptian had stood. Then his eyes sprang open again, wide and staring. Billy's jaw twitched.

"For those who dare disturb my tomb, Remember you have sealed your doom!" he chanted.

Charley's hands clenched into fists as the message from beyond the grave vibrated inside her soul. The ripples spread out through 44 Morningside Place, until it seemed that every timber, every brick resonated with the mummy's curse.

Cowley was rooted to the spot. The blood had drained from his cheeks, leaving his face as grey and cold as the grave.

The message delivered, Billy dropped to the ground.

Lifeless. Charley rushed to him. Leaning over the side of her chair, she placed one hand on his cheek, rousing him gently. "I'm here, partner," she said.

Billy woke with a gasp and sat bolt upright. He looked confused, as if he was struggling to make sense of the world around him.

"Billy," said Charley soothingly. "It's me, Charley."

Billy stared at her as if they had never met, then, with another blink, the light of recognition dawned. "It's real," said Billy. "The mummy, the curse, all of it."

Charley nodded. She was a scientist at heart but she was also a S.C.R.E.A.M. detective. She knew that science had only begun to scratch the surface of the mysteries of the universe.

"We can solve this," she said, but her voice wavered slightly as she said it.

"Yes," said Billy, squeezing her hand, hearing the tremble in her voice. "I'm afraid too."

CHAPTER TEN

HEART OF DARKNESS

"Blast," said Charley. Back in her room after the tour of the house, she was rifling through her suitcase for the third time with growing irritation. But it wasn't there. She felt a sudden pang of emptiness.

It was silly, Charley knew – it was only a small piece of silver. But it was something she treasured and she always carried it with her. Her father had given it to her and when she held it in her hand, she imagined that he was near.

"Blast and damn!"

Where was it? She remembered having it at the hotel

because she'd shoved it into her bag when they had to get out in such a hurry.

"What's the matter?" asked Billy, arriving in the doorway.

"I can't find my watch."

"The little pendant you wear round your neck? You had it on the train, I'm sure." Billy frowned. "It'll come to light," he said hopefully.

He was about to help her look when Doogie knocked on the door. "If you'd care to follow me," he said, "Sir Gordon has rearranged the conservatory so that ye have an area to work in."

Charley smiled. "Excellent," she said. "Be a good chap and carry these down for me too, please." She indicated her precious microscope and the bags containing some of her books and chemicals. "I collected a rather interesting sample at Lady Fitzpatrick's and I'm keen to unravel its secrets."

"Oooh," said Billy. "I'm intrigued."

"It's that tiny strand of cloth fibre I told you about."

"Uh-huh. I'm slightly less excited now."

Doogie hesitated. He still hadn't picked up Charley's microscope.

"Is there a problem?" Charley asked.

"No, miss, but...I don't think ye'll be needin' it."

"Why ever not?"

"His Lordship has a surprise for ye. It's best if ye just come and look."

They returned to the lift. Cowley was out, walking Wellington apparently. Doogie closed the doors and, with the usual creaking and groaning of the suspension cables, the lift juddered down to the ground floor.

"This way," said Doogie, bouncing ahead of them down the corridor. Charley paused at a huge portrait of Sir Gordon. She smiled. Though it was definitely Sir Gordon, the artist had been very kind, making His Lordship taller and much slimmer than he was in real life. "He looks a real Skinny Malinky long legs," Doogie chuckled.

When they had wiped the grins from their faces, Doogie took them the rest of the way, finally stopping at a set of double doors. Doogie turned the handle and flung them wide. "Welcome to the crime lab!"

Charley gasped. She didn't know what she'd been expecting, but it certainly wasn't this. Like every room in 44 Morningside Place, Sir Gordon's conservatory was full of surprises.

The two detectives were surrounded on all sides by exotic plants from around the world. Most gardeners were content with an orange tree and a few orchids. Clearly not Sir Gordon. Some of the plants were vast, with knotted trunks and huge waxy leaves. Vines climbed up the walls, and hung in loops from the ceiling. Dotted here and there through the undergrowth were the ghostly white shapes of statues – Greek beauties that had been frozen in time, furry moss clinging to their perfect faces like beards.

Charley spotted the huge white trumpet-shaped flowers of the *datura*. She brought her nose close and drank in the heavenly aroma. Billy cupped another flower, like a bright red mouth surrounded by thin spiky leaves, pulling it towards his nose for a sniff.

"I wouldn't if I were you," warned Charley.

"It's just a plant," shrugged Billy. "How dangerous can a plant be?"

A fat fly buzzed over, drawn by the strange flower's sickly scent. It landed and quickly found that its six tiny feet were stuck. Before it could escape the plant had closed around the poor insect, trapping it inside a red velvet cage.

"It's a Venus flytrap," said Charley. "A carnivorous plant."

"A plant that eats meat?" said Billy. "Lovely."

The plants stirred suddenly overhead and, looking up, they saw a flash of blue and yellow as a huge bird came squawking and shrieking out of the canopy of leaves.

"What the—?" said Billy, ducking as the bird swooped past, its beak clacking.

"Ach, don't worry, that's just Queen Victoria," said Doogie. "She's a parrot."

"God save me!" Queen Victoria screeched from somewhere overhead. "Show us your bloomers!"

"Nobody knows who taught her to say that," said Doogie, a little sheepishly.

"I imagine it's a complete mystery," said Billy, giving the young lad a knowing look. "Any other animals that we should know about?"

"Only Prince Albert," said Doogie. "He's a snake."

"Of course he is," said Billy. "Stands to reason."

"There," said Charley softly. Billy followed the line of her gaze until he spotted the coiled shape, wrapped around a branch. It was a vivid green with a yellow diamond pattern down its scaly back.

"That's a big snake," said Billy.

"A green boa," said Charley, "quite a beautiful specimen actually."

"If you say so," said Billy. Prince Albert looked at Billy and poked out a forked tongue. It hissed menacingly and Billy took a step back. "I feel like I'm in a zoo. In what way is this a crime lab?"

"In this way," said Doogie proudly. "Sir Gordon had Mr Cowley working half the night to get this ready."

They followed the path through the conservatory and found that an area had been cleared for them. A blackboard had been installed, accompanied by a new box of chalk. Positioned next to that was a large map of Edinburgh on an easel and an extensive selection of reference books. There were also chairs, tables, pencils, paper, notepads, ink pads, a magnifying glass, reading lamps, an impressive chemistry set, Sir Gordon's own camera and, to Charley's delight, the finest microscope she had ever seen.

"Look at this!" she said.

"Look at this!" said Billy, heading for a side table where a tea urn was bubbling merrily and a plate of biscuits had been arranged. "Sir Gordon really has thought of everything," he said, spraying crumbs. He was bringing a second biscuit to his lips when Queen Victoria swooped down and snatched it right out of his hand.

"She does that," said Doogie.

Billy glared at the bird and shoved another biscuit into his mouth whole; he wasn't taking any risks this time.

Now that they weren't in the thick jungle part of the conservatory and were far enough away from Prince Albert, Billy could see that this would be a good place to work. The windows let in a clear light and a vent provided a pleasant breeze. There was even an ornamental pool with a fountain in the middle and beautiful fish swimming in slow circles. The tinkling of the water was very relaxing, almost like music. Although the effect was somewhat spoiled by the glass tank nearby which held some enormous hairy spiders and a selection of other equally horrible scuttling things. Billy shivered; he didn't like bugs.

"Don't worry," Charley said, reading the look on his face. "None of those spiders or scorpions could actually kill you. Oh, except for those yellow ones. They're deathstalker scorpions. They *are* deadly. One sting is all it would take."

"Where is Sir Gordon, by the way?" Billy changed the subject, and edged away from the crawling nasties. "We haven't seen him since we arrived."

"His Lordship has business in town," said Doogie. "He said something about buying a gun. He's afraid... We all are."

CHAPTER ELEVEN

MASTER AND SERVANT

By flickering candlelight, in his secret, dark place, the Sandman was busy. His eyes narrowed to slits as he concentrated on his task. Egyptian magick as powerful as this couldn't be rushed. Preparation was everything.

He had bathed in scalding hot water and dressed in the white linen robes of a Lector Priest – an Egyptian magician. The braziers were lit and the coals were glowing red-hot. With ceremony, the Sandman placed an earthenware bowl on the coals and then carefully lowered a block of wax into the dish. Within seconds the wax had softened and was becoming a bubbling soup.

Using tongs, he removed the bowl from the coals and poured the molten wax into a wooden mould.

The Sandman smiled as the wax ran into the recesses and the shape became clear. Two arms, two legs, a body, a head. He was making a figure, a little wax person. But not just any person…this doll would have a name.

The wax quickly started to harden and while it was still soft enough for him to shape with his hands, the Sandman tipped up the mould and set to work. He smoothed the limbs and added features to the blank face; a nose, two holes for eyes. It was crude and lumpy but still easily identifiable as a human figure. The Sandman paused. A sheen of sweat covered his face and he wiped it away nervously. There was always a risk when casting a spell… He had to do this right. One wrong ingredient, the wrong action, the wrong word…and the result would be disastrous. Possibly fatal.

In his hours of study, the Sandman had learned that Egyptian magick – *Heka* – had two components. The physical: the ingredients, the ritual actions. And the spoken: the words of power.

Using an ornate knife, the Sandman cut a small slit for a mouth then, leaning over, he breathed into it. "Breath of my breath," he said quietly.

A groaning sound behind him made the hairs on his neck stand on end. The Sandman paused in his labours and looked over his shoulder. It was the mummy, standing motionless, waiting for its next command.

The Sandman crossed the chamber and stood in front of the creature. Once upon a time the mummy had been a king, but now it was *his* servant. It felt good to be the one with the power for a change.

"You're angry, aren't you?" said the Sandman. "Good! I'm angry too."

The mummy stirred, the moaning becoming a fierce growl. The bandaged feet shuffled and the arms began to rise from its sides.

"Halt!" ordered the Sandman. He stepped closer until his face was level with the mummy's. The Sandman stared into the pits where the eyes had been. He had grown used to the disgusting perfume of decay which filled the air wherever the undead creature went. For the Sandman, this had become the smell of victory.

"I wear the Eye of Horus," said the Sandman, stroking the gold pendant at his throat. "You go when I say 'go'; you are mine to command."

The mummy retreated and the Sandman returned to his wax doll.

It needed one finishing touch.

The Sandman picked up a large curved bone; an enormous tooth. It was a hippo tusk engraved with hieroglyphs. It had been a gift from a stupid man who didn't understand its real value.

It was an Egyptian wand.

With quiet satisfaction, the Sandman reached into the leather pouch at his belt and pulled out a polished brass button. Then he pressed the tip of the wand into the warm chest of the wax doll and slit it open like a surgeon. When the hole was big enough, he pushed the button inside and closed up the wound again, burying it inside.

Finally the Sandman unrolled a papyrus scroll. It had been written by a priest of Osiris, the Egyptian god of the afterlife, the underworld and the dead.

The Sandman cleared his throat and broke the silence.

"Looking, you will not see.

Searching, you shall not find me.

Seek me and all you gain

Is entry to a world of...*pain*."

The Sandman turned the wax doll over in his hands. It had a fat round head and a swollen belly with a button inside. For some reason it made the Sandman laugh.

"You can't say I didn't warn you," he chuckled.

CHAPTER TWELVE

NIGHT NIGHT, SWEET SCREAMS

Charley lifted her face from the microscope and rolled her shoulders. She had been bent over her samples for the best part of an hour and she ached. Billy knew that his partner was in discomfort; she often was.

"What have you found?" he asked gently.

"All the sand samples match," she said. "Pure white Saharan. And, as I suspected, the cotton fibre I collected from the safe could have been made yesterday."

Billy furrowed his brow. "So what does that mean? Is the mummy a fake after all?"

"The mummy that attacked us seemed real enough

and Lady Fitzpatrick's description was very vivid." Charley shook her head. "I've left out the best part... The fresh white cotton had traces of black ash on one side."

Billy rubbed his arm, which felt bruised after the mummy's crushing grip. "So if an *old* mummy is wearing *new* bandages—"

"Then it *can't* be working alone," finished Charley. "Someone repaired it."

"You mean," said Billy, "that we're looking for a 'daddy' too?"

"You think you're so funny, don't you?"

"It's a blessing..." said Billy modestly. "And a curse."

"Mostly a curse, from where I'm sitting." Charley smiled, although she was so tired that it turned into a yawn. "How about you, Billy? Is your sixth sense telling you anything?"

"I'm sorry," said Billy. "My skill isn't like yours. Your brain works every time you want it to, but my...*ability* isn't as reliable as that. I wish it was. I wish I could just point the way straight to the end of the trail."

"Where would be the fun in that?"

"To tell you the truth, Charley, there are so many things whispering to me in this odd house that I can't hear anything clearly at all."

"44 Morningside Place has to be one of the weirdest crime scenes we've ever been called to," Charley agreed.

"Imagine that you're standing in a doorway, half in the room and half out," Billy went on, doing his best to put into words something he didn't really understand himself. "It's like I've got one foot in this world – the one that we can see and feel with our natural bodies – and the other in a spirit realm; an invisible world that's just as real as this one."

"That must feel…*strange*."

"Strange isn't even close," said Billy. "It's as if I'm trying to see through a window that hasn't been washed in centuries, or attempting to hear one voice in a crowded street." He rubbed the back of his neck thoughtfully. "Hardly anything that I see or hear or smell from the other side is clear at all. I get pictures or impressions of things, flashes of insight, and Sir Gordon's house is so cluttered with objects that it's almost impossible for me to cut through the noise.

"Just walking down the hallway, for example, I know that the boxful of finger bones belonged to a shaman. I can see him clearly, rolling the bones in dust and reading the future in them. Since we went into Sir Gordon's Egyptian hall, all I can taste is the desert. I can still feel the sand blowing on my face, carried on the winds of time…"

Charley looked at her partner's face, getting a glimpse of the burden he carried.

"Some of the dead people in the photographs that Sir Gordon likes taking have been talking to me, shouting their names, or mumbling incoherently…" Billy's face clouded slightly. "It's not easy."

He turned to Charley. "I also know that owl in the study hates being dead and stuffed but really enjoys playing the banjo." Billy's face cracked into a grin.

"You made that up," said Charley.

"Only the bit about the owl," he confessed. A dinner gong rang, summoning them both to the table. "Come on, I'm starving."

Dinner came and went. Five courses. Mrs Fudge, the cook, had prepared Scotch broth, smoked salmon, good Scottish beef with roast potatoes, followed by raspberry blancmange and a cheeseboard. They ate quietly, watched over by Mr Cowley. Plus a row of shrunken heads in a display case and the glassy eyes of a stuffed penguin riding a bicycle.

Wellington seemed spooked. He kept whining and was snuffling round their feet under the table, as if he was hiding from something. Charley slipped a slice of beef to him and Wellington took it eagerly, his rough tongue lapping at her fingers. Charley gave him another slice; she wasn't really in the mood for eating. She was in worse discomfort than usual and her head felt strange. She'd overdone it probably, and she couldn't wait for her bed.

The food was all delicious, but the meal had been an awkward experience. The atmosphere in 44 Morningside Place was tense. Two more servants had handed in their notice, and the remaining staff were on edge, as if expecting disaster. The weight of the curse on their minds, thought Charley. Even the ticking of the clock, usually such a reassuring sound, only made her feel that time was running out.

They hardly spoke a word. A combination of weariness and worry had taken its toll. Sir Gordon was sweating even more heavily than usual, and once or twice Charley had spotted him wince slightly during dinner. Probably heartburn, she guessed.

Sir Gordon pushed his plate aside. "Take this away, Cowley," he said. "My nerves are in tatters, I have no appetite at all." Charley noticed how his waistcoat was straining to hold in his fat stomach. There was even a button missing! But she kept her thoughts to herself.

"Coffee, sir?" Cowley asked, bringing a steaming silver pot from the dresser. "After-dinner chocolates?"

"Just the one, to be sociable," said Sir Gordon, popping a chocolate straight into the pink round hole of his mouth and putting two more on a side plate. His Lordship belched loudly and then covered his mouth in embarrassment.

Charley and Billy made their excuses and headed off for bed, leaving Sir Gordon with the port decanter and one more slice of cheese. Possibly two. And some grapes. And then perhaps a brandy.

The ride up in the lift was silent. The lift gates opened and Charley and Billy paused in the corridor before heading for their bedrooms.

"You all right, Duchess?" Billy asked. "You look done in."

"Fine," said Charley, even as a twinge of pain stabbed at her temple. She winced and raised her fingers to her forehead. "Just a headache."

"Can I get you anything?"

"No," she said, waving away his help. "Cowley has

100

left a jug of water in my room, I had a glass earlier. Give me a good night's sleep and I'll be tickety-boo in the morning."

Billy hovered; she could tell he was concerned about her.

"Go!" Charley insisted. "I'm fine."

But she wasn't.

Charley's head was spinning by the time she closed her bedroom door behind her. Her wheelchair felt as if it was made of lead and her strength was failing fast; she barely had the energy to reach the bedside cabinet. She made a fumbling attempt to pour some water to clear her head, but the jug slipped straight through her fingers. The room was a blur. *I just need to lie down,* she told herself.

She pushed down on the arms of her chair. Shakily she heaved herself upright and tried to shuffle towards the bed. Cold sweat ran down her forehead and another wave of dizziness washed over her.

The bed loomed above her. It was impossibly large, a mountain of eiderdown which she would never be able to climb, not even in a million years. The terrible whirling inside her head grew worse and, just as quickly as it had grown, the bed now seemed to disappear into the distance, until it was a tiny speck on the horizon. Charley swayed. Her head weighed more than her whole body and there was nothing she could do to stop it from dragging her down to the floor.

The pain in her skull was incredible. An awful hammering that screwed her left eye shut with agony. The headache was so sharp it was as if it had been nailed there.

Billy! Help! She was screaming on the inside but wasn't sure whether the words even made it as far as her lips.

As the headache stabbed again, Charley passed out.

CHAPTER THIRTEEN

THE STING IN THE TAIL

In his bedroom Billy splashed some water on his face and changed into his nightclothes. There was a fire in the grate and he stood in the comforting warmth while he slipped into his nightshirt. He climbed into bed and pulled up the sheet. Billy was dog-tired, having spent most of the previous night fighting the fire at the hotel. He should have fallen asleep instantly but he couldn't relax in 44 Morningside Place.

Sir Gordon's weird and wonderful collections were a distraction, a background noise to something bigger and darker and infinitely more powerful…

All of the servants were saying it: *This house is cursed.*

Billy felt his skin begin to crawl and in spite of the warmth of the fire an icy terror came over him. He suddenly had the most awful feeling that he was not alone in the room.

Tucked up in bed, Billy peered suspiciously into every shadow… Was there someone behind the curtains? Had he left the wardrobe door ajar like that? Could there be something under the bed?

The creeping fear grew worse. Billy could almost feel it making its way up his chest.

That was when he realized the worst. There really *was* something creeping up his chest.

With trembling fingers, Billy drew back the sheet and saw a huge evil-looking creature scuttling up his body. A scorpion! With pincers raised and poisonous tail coiled to strike!

Billy didn't dare move. Even breathing seemed risky. He could feel the scratch of the scorpion's feet through his nightshirt. Its armoured body was golden yellow. Sharp jaws snapped and hissed. The fat bulb of the stinger was poised on the end of the segmented tail, a drop of poison glistening at the tip… *One sting was all it would take.*

Billy struggled to keep a lid on his fear. Goosebumps

rose along his arms. *Why did it have to be the deathstalker?* Trying to keep his body as still as possible, Billy ran through his options. If he was quick he might be able to sweep the scorpion off, get some space between him and it. But he would have to be *very* quick... The scorpion advanced further up Billy's body, almost as if it had realized that a plan was being hatched against it.

Billy stole a glance sideways to see if there was anything on the bedside table that he might be able to use as a weapon. There was a candle, a glass of water and a Bible...a nice, *heavy* Bible.

Billy quickly ran through the motions in his mind... reach out with his right hand, pick up the book, sweep the scorpion on the floor with a single blow, throw back the bedsheet with his left hand, jump out of bed and find something to finish the horrible thing off before it regained its senses and attacked again...

Billy inched his fingers towards the Bible just as the scorpion raised its claws... *Here we go!*

He snatched up the book and brought it across his body with every ounce of his strength, sending the scorpion flying. Without even waiting to see where the creature fell, Billy leaped up. He ran to the end of the bed, jumped off and grabbed the iron poker from the fireplace. He felt better now that he had a weapon in his hand, although he was very aware that his bare feet were vulnerable.

The only light in the room came from the flickering embers in the grate. The scorpion was nowhere to be seen. There was a rug in front of the fire, and another small rug beside the bed, but the rest of the floor was naked wooden boards. Billy listened and heard the *click click click* of eight feet scuttling towards him at incredible speed.

Billy spun around, desperate to see where the deathstalker was coming from. He thought he saw a flicker of movement beside the leg of the bed and he lashed out with the poker, striking the floorboard so hard that the wood splintered. If the scorpion had been there it wasn't now… He heard the scratching of its feet again and he spun round once more, this time hitting the floor behind him with another deafening crack. *Damn, it was quick!*

Billy backed away until he was up against the wall. At least that way he couldn't be sneaked up on from behind.

Footsteps approached from the corridor outside. "Are ye all right?" called a voice.

"Doogie! Get in here quick, I need your help!"

The lad poked his head around the door. He looked

even younger dressed in his nightshirt. Billy reached down with his free hand. He grabbed the steel tongs that were used to put coals onto the fire and threw them to Doogie. "Catch."

"Is there a wee mouse?" asked Doogie.

"Something a bit more vicious than that – look!" He pointed with his poker. "There it is!"

"I hate those beasties!" said Doogie, his face showing more than a flicker of fear.

Nevertheless, both boys launched themselves as one. Billy managed to catch the deathstalker a glancing blow, knocking it over onto its back. Its legs kicked in the air frantically as it tried to right itself again and Doogie moved in with the tongs, grabbing it by the tail and picking it up. The scorpion continued to thrash, its pincers snapping at empty air.

"Whatever you do, don't let it go!" yelled Billy. Part of him wanted to throw the vicious creature into the fire, but he couldn't blame an animal for simply following its instinct. "Drop it in the wastepaper basket," said Billy, bending down to pick up the fallen Bible. "On three. One…two…*three.*"

Doogie released the tongs and the scorpion fell into the wire cage of the waiting basket. It seemed stunned for a second, and then started to climb up towards freedom with lightning speed. It would have made it too, if Billy hadn't blocked the way, trapping the deathstalker inside the bin with the heavy book.

They relaxed, both breathing heavily from their efforts.

"It was in my bed," said Billy.

"It must have escaped from the tank in the conservatory," said Doogie.

"And if one could get out, then there might be more of them on the loose… *Charley!*" He was running as he shouted her name.

Billy burst into Charley's room and found his partner writhing on the floor. He dropped to his knees beside her and cradled her head in his lap. Her face was twisted with pain. Her skin was cold and clammy. "Duchess," he said anxiously, wiping the sweat from her brow.

Her face was turning blue…

"See if there are any more of those scorpions lurking," Billy ordered Doogie. "I'm getting Charley out of here."

Billy scooped Charley up in his arms and took her into the relative safety of the corridor, where there were fewer places for a scorpion or a tarantula or goodness knows what to hide.

Lowering Charley down again, Billy patted her cheek with the palm of his hand, trying to bring her round. "Charley, it's me, Billy. Have you been stung? Where are you hurt? Charley…" Billy refused to let the panic show in his voice. "Duchess," he urged. "Wake up, please."

"Eh? What…what's going on?" Charley's voice was slurred. "Where am I?"

"You had me scared," said Billy.

"I'm…fine," said Charley, although her pained expression suggested she was anything but "fine". Awkwardly she hauled herself up into a sitting position and spotted Doogie standing in the doorway to her room, waving an iron poker.

"No sign," said Doogie.

"What *is* going on?" said Charley.

"That's what we're trying to find—"

A scream rang out, echoing down the corridor.

"Sir Gordon!" yelled Doogie, setting off at a sprint.

"Leave me!" said Charley, as Billy hesitated. "*GO!*"

Two seconds later and Billy was at Doogie's side outside His Lordship's room. Billy turned the handle but the door wouldn't budge. "Locked."

"Sir Gordon! Sir Gordon!" Doogie banged on the door. Another scream pierced the night.

"We'll have to break it down," said Billy.

They flung their shoulders against the wood and – with a splintering *crack!* – the lock broke and Billy and Doogie fell into the room.

"We're too late," said Doogie, as he saw Sir Gordon's body sprawled across the bed, as white and blubbery as a beached whale – if beached whales wore stripy nightshirts. "He's dead."

CHAPTER FOURTEEN

SMELLS LIKE TROUBLE

But Sir Gordon wasn't dead – Billy realized this as soon as he drew close and His Lordship lifted one buttock to release a fart of monstrous proportions.

"Sir Gordon," said Billy, "you were screaming. What happened?"

His Lordship wiped his perspiring brow on the bedsheet. "I was in agony," he said, gently stroking his fat belly. "Never felt pain like it. It was as if someone was jabbing at my stomach with a red-hot poker."

"And now?" said Billy. "How do you feel now?"

"Still dreadful," said Sir Gordon, farting again

and wafting his nightshirt.

"I'll fetch a doctor for you immediately, sir," said Cowley, standing framed in the doorway. The butler lacked his usual dignity, dressed in a nightshirt and with a long nightcap pulled down tight over his head.

"If ye can find one who isn't afraid of the mummy's curse," whispered Doogie.

A grandfather clock chimed three in the morning, signalling the start of the bleakest, loneliest, longest hour of what had already been a desperate night. Not a soul in 44 Morningside Place was sleeping. The mummy's curse had murdered sleep.

Doctor Cushing fussed over Sir Gordon, prescribing a pinch of gunpowder stirred into a glass of warm soapy water to be drunk as a cure for the violent stomach pain. Cowley fussed over the household staff. The two parlourmaids were leaving and there was nothing he could say to persuade them to stay. Doogie fussed over Charley, although she was adamant that the headache had gone now as quickly as it had come. Charley fussed over the case notes, reading and rereading every page. And Billy? Well, Billy went down to the kitchen and made some hot chocolate. Then he sat alone at the table, the cup in both hands while he drank and tried to forget the deathstalker. They'd checked the scorpion tank in the conservatory and the lid was slightly ajar, so the nasty thing must have escaped by accident. But accident or not, it still could have ended his life with one whip of its tail.

A pale sun eventually rose over Edinburgh, bringing light but no warmth. Washed and dressed, Sir Gordon, Charley and Billy all sat round the breakfast table. Wellington lay under it. Cowley and Beth, the last remaining downstairs maid, were on hand to serve tea, hot coffee, toast with strawberry jam or bitter marmalade, porridge, bacon, sausages, black pudding, eggs (scrambled, fried, poached and boiled), kippers and kedgeree.

Charley eventually chose a simple boiled egg. She lined up some toast soldiers on the side of her plate and then took great pleasure in cracking the egg open with her spoon.

"On which," said Billy, "how's your head?"

"Fine, thank you," said Charley, waving his concern away. "Although it was terrible at the time." She poured some milk into her tea and gave it a stir. "Oh dear," she said, wrinkling her nose as she saw the creamy blobs spinning on the surface. "I think the milk has gone off."

Beth dropped the tray she was carrying and screamed. "It's the curse!" she shrieked and fled from the dining room in tears, Cowley stalking after her.

"My entire household is crumbling around me," said Sir Gordon. He sounded like a little lost six year old. "You still love me though, don't you, Wellington?" He took the bacon off his plate and the dog gobbled it appreciatively, licking his master's hand.

Charley had brought one of her reference books to the table. Finding the illustrated page that she was looking for, she pushed it over to Billy. "Look familiar?"

Billy instantly recognized the hideous creatures from his vision. "What are they?"

"Egyptian gods," said Charley. "Sekhmet the lioness, Sobek the crocodile and Anubis the jackal."

"Does that crocodile bloke remind you of anyone?" said Billy, munching through a sausage. "Like our friend back at the railway station lurking in the shadows?"

"I only saw a silhouette," said Charley, "but it's possible, I suppose."

"Almost enough to put me off my breakfast," said Billy. "But not quite."

Billy had chosen some lighter reading, and was flicking through the newspaper while he tackled what was left of his sausage and eggs. But he stopped with a piece of fried egg halfway to his mouth when he spotted an advert at the bottom of the page. "Listen to this…"

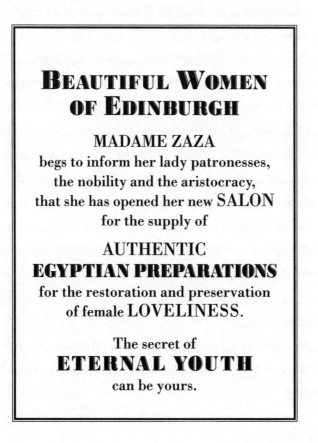

BEAUTIFUL WOMEN OF EDINBURGH

MADAME ZAZA
begs to inform her lady patronesses,
the nobility and the aristocracy,
that she has opened her new SALON
for the supply of

AUTHENTIC
EGYPTIAN PREPARATIONS
for the restoration and preservation
of female LOVELINESS.

The secret of
ETERNAL YOUTH
can be yours.

"I think I should check it out," said Billy.

Charley raised an eyebrow. "Shouldn't *I* be the one to investigate a beauty parlour?"

"It's a tough job," said Billy, "but someone's got to do it."

"So nothing to do with surrounding yourself with 'female loveliness' then?"

"Sadly not," said Billy. "I've got a hunch that the Flint family are mixed up in this. I've got a dodgy cousin who tried something very similar in London. He might be out of prison by now."

"I thought you were having me on when you said he was from a family of criminals, Miss Steel!" spluttered Sir Gordon.

"I wish she was," said Billy, "but I'm related to at least forty-five burglars; three safe crackers; one rather brilliant forger; a slightly mad arsonist; more sneak thieves, thugs and pickpockets than you can shake a truncheon at…"

Sir Gordon's face went white at the thought of such villainy and he tucked his gold fob watch deeper into his pocket.

"But the funniest thing is that *I'm* the black sheep of the family."

"Billy's the one they talk about in whispers," Charley added.

"Why on earth is that?" said Sir Gordon.

"Nothing on earth, actually," said Billy cryptically.

"Eh? I'm lost," said Sir Gordon.

"My *un*earthly talent has a habit of upsetting people," said Billy. "When you tell people that you can see angels and demons and everything in between, they tend to think you're…strange, treat you as an outcast. Mum packed me off to be a priest and that was where Luther Sparkwell found me – I was casting out an unclean spirit, he was chasing a spectre…"

"The old, old story," chuckled Charley. "Boy meets ghoul!"

"Anyway, Luther recruited me to the new police department he was setting up and, well, here I am."

"Right," said Charley, patting her lips with her napkin. "Evil villains don't just catch themselves. You check out Madame ZaZa and while you're doing that, I want to go back to the scene of the first burglary, see what I can find there."

Charley turned to His Lordship, who was on his third helping of porridge despite his stomach pains. "Don't worry, Sir Gordon, S.C.R.E.A.M. are on the case."

CHAPTER FIFTEEN

COME INTO MY PARLOUR

Billy found Madame ZaZa's beauty parlour easily enough. It certainly didn't test his detective skills.

The street was not in the most exclusive neighbourhood and the house itself had seen better days. The windows were dirty. The paint was peeling. Billy sniffed the air and caught a waft of heady perfume that was so thick and sweet it almost made him gag. But what really gave it away were the two muscular men standing on either side of the doorway. They were naked apart from Egyptian headdresses, short leather kilts and sandals. They held spears, which on closer inspection appeared

118

to be broom handles with fish knives tied to the top with string, and painted gold.

Billy smiled. None of this came as a surprise. He was one of the Flint family; he knew a scam when he saw one. He wet the palm of his hand and smoothed down his hair. He wanted to look his best for any "lovelies" he might find in the course of his investigation. Billy approached the door with a bounce in his step. "Hello, gents," he said. "Madame ZaZa at home?"

"She don't see no one without an appointment," said the first guard.

"She'll see me," said Billy, flipping open his wallet to reveal his police badge.

The guard seemed a lot less cocky all of a sudden. "Er...I'll go and see if she's in."

"So you can warn her and she can leg it out the back? I think not," said Billy. "I'll see myself in, thanks."

Billy left the two bewildered guards behind and went in before they could react. Inside, the decor was just as shabby as the outside, but that didn't seem to have put off Madame ZaZa's clients. The waiting room was full. Perched on chairs and balanced on an old chaise longue were over a dozen expensively-dressed women. Billy felt rather out of place; a fish out of water. He also felt a pang of disappointment: the "beauties" here looked like his grandma.

One smiled at him. Two of her front teeth were missing. He tried hard not to notice the wiry bristles sprouting across her jaw. "You can sit by me, sonny," she said, shuffling up and patting the seat. Billy shuddered. *Not by the hair on your chinny chin chin.*

"Madame ZaZa's is shut for the day," said Billy, holding his police badge up for them all to see. "You nice ladies need to go."

The ladies looked confused.

"Now," said Billy, shooing them towards the door with outspread arms, as if he was rounding up sheep. There was a lot of clicking of tongues and a few muttered *"well I never"*s but Billy didn't hang around to listen. He pushed open the door that led into Madame ZaZa's inner sanctum and marched straight in.

The room had been decorated to resemble the interior of a desert tent. Or at least a romantic fantasy of one. The ceiling and walls were hung with silk sheets, the ornate furniture had been given a lick of gold paint and an Egyptian rug covered the floor. There were two women in the room: the client was sitting in a chair and the other, Madame ZaZa presumably, was standing beside her with her back to the door. Even seeing Madame ZaZa from behind, Billy recognized her. She wore a long white robe which reached to the floor, tied at the waist with a gold chain. An ornamental collar hung around her neck, studded with gems. Madame ZaZa's hair was as black as night. It was fashioned into small tight braids, hanging in a bob above her surprisingly broad shoulders.

The client in the chair spotted Billy and opened her mouth to speak, sending a spiderweb of cracks through the thick white mixture that had been painted over her face.

"You must say nussink," said Madame ZaZa, as she continued to apply the foul-smelling mixture with what appeared to be an old paintbrush.

The client in the chair looked really alarmed now and was pointing over Madame ZaZa's shoulder, straight at Billy.

"Do not disturb yourself, my darlink," said Madame ZaZa, in her thick foreign accent which seemed to come from everywhere and nowhere in particular. "Ozzerwize the formula will not work its magic." Her customer was still pointing and with more than a touch of anger in her heavily made-up eyes, Madame ZaZa turned to see what the fuss was about. "I told you that I am never to be disturbed when I am wiz a client."

Her gaze fell on Billy.

"Chuff me," said Madame ZaZa gruffly from behind the veil which covered her mouth, and the accent dropped completely. "Billy Flint, as I live and breathe."

"We need to talk," said Billy.

Madame ZaZa turned to her client. "Fetch yer coat," she said, now sounding like an East Ender who had never been anywhere more exotic than Millwall. "I'll have to finish your treatment later, love." Then, quick as a flash, Madame ZaZa hitched up her robe past her hairy knees and made a dash for the door.

However Billy had been expecting Madame ZaZa to be as slippery as an eel. He nipped in quickly, stuck his leg out and sent Madame Zaza tumbling. Her veil fell off and her wig slipped, revealing a shaven head gleaming underneath.

As the distressed client made her own escape, Billy stood over the fallen figure of Madame ZaZa. He shook his head. "Up to your old tricks again, eh, Tosher?"

CHAPTER SIXTEEN

RAZOR'S EDGE

Charley's back ached even more than usual and it hadn't helped that she had slept so badly. No matter which way she sat inside the carriage this morning she couldn't seem to relieve the pain. Doogie had given her a cushion but little good it did her. Her lips tightened as another twinge hit, but she didn't have time to think about it; she had a case to solve.

Just as the carriage was leaving, a messenger had arrived with a telegram from London. It was from Luther Sparkwell.

POST OFFICE TELEGRAPHS   S.C.R.E.A.M.

TOP SECRET S.C.R.E.A.M. COMMUNICATIONS FOR URGENT DISPATCH

Zombie captured

Now Banshee loose in Regents Park

You're on your own

Try not to get killed

Sparkwell

"I'll do my best," she muttered as the zebras drew her away.

Charley pulled out her notebook and looked at the hieroglyphics that she had been able to translate so far. She had copied them in the order that Billy had found them, including the gaps where the sand had been swept away.

A sceptre or wand, an eye, a man with his arm outstretched, then a gap, then a hippo's head. The sceptre stood for "power" or "strength" or "authority". That was one of the more straightforward symbols. The trouble was that hieroglyphs could have more than one meaning, depending on the context. Charley scratched her head with her pencil, and her brows knitted together in thought. The eye might mean "make" or "do" or "see" or "watch" or "be watchful" or "be blind". Or just "eye". The man could mean "to call" or "servant" or simply "man".

Then there was the hippo. At least she thought it was a hippo. Animal symbols were especially tricky to translate, with numerous odd meanings. She mentally ran through the list. What did this hippo stand for, she wondered. A moment? An instant? A snap of the fingers? An actual hippo?

Charley was still lost in thought when the carriage arrived at the scene of the first burglary. Lady Marigold Tiffin's house had been burgled the night after Sir Gordon's disastrous mummy party. It was a majestic building befitting someone of Lady T's wealth but if some homes seemed to glow with the warmth, love and laughter that could be found inside, then this stately home was a place of quiet desperation. It stood alone in an acre of woodland, and although the sun was high in the grey sky, the tall, dark pine trees did everything they could to shut out the light.

The coachman helped Charley down and into her wheelchair. All around them the pines seemed to whisper to each other, their dry branches creaking. No birds sang in this wood. No children played hide and seek here. The zebras seemed skittish and uneasy, whinnying and pawing the ground with their hooves.

Charley grabbed her wheels and propelled her chair forwards along the gravel path. Her arms were muscular and they needed to be. Her father had christened her Charlotte *Fortitude* Steel – strength really was her middle name.

Aching, Charley reached the front door and heaved down on the bell pull. A bell jangled somewhere inside the house but there were no other signs of life from within. Charley rang again, gave it another minute and then decided she would try the back entrance.

The gravel path extended right round the lonely old house and Charley made agonizing progress. Eventually she reached the rear entrance. There was no bell on the back door, so she banged on it with her knuckles. She spotted a flicker of movement at a window; a fat face looking out for a second, then it was gone.

"Open up," Charley called. "Police!"

Footsteps reluctantly approached and the door opened.

A round-faced woman stood there, her puffy cheeks full of annoyance. "What d'you want?"

"I am Charlotte Steel, S.C.R.E.A.M. squad, and I want to speak to the mistress of the house."

"You can't," said the woman. "She's out."

"I'll wait for her to get back," said Charley, pushing herself into the house in defiance of this rude woman.

"You'll have a long wait then, darling," the woman purred. "She's gone to London. I don't expect to see her back for months."

That explained a lot, Charley thought. With Lady Tiffin gone away, no doubt to rebuild her shattered nerves after her ordeal, the servants had the place to themselves. "Then I will have to talk with *you*," said Charley, allowing an icy note into her voice.

"Me?"

"You are Mrs Whisker, aren't you?" She studied the housekeeper; the fat face, the fuzz of hairs on her upper lip. "Violet Ermintrude Whisker? Thirty-nine years old, born in County Durham, previously employed as a housemaid to General Thaddeus Shermann, one previous conviction for theft." Charley paused. "Left the General's employment after some sort of scandal involving missing silver cutlery. You are *that* Mrs Whisker, aren't you?"

The woman was flustered. "How do you know all that?"

"I'm a detective," said Charley. "It is my business to know everything about everybody. Now let's sit together and talk politely, but first I'd like a pot of Earl Grey with lemon, not milk. Run along and fetch it, would you?"

Now that the beauty parlour was deserted, Madame ZaZa abandoned her disguise completely. As Billy had suspected all along, Madame ZaZa was not Egyptian. And not a madame either. Madame ZaZa was Tosher Flint. One of Billy's numerous cousins from the vast criminal clan of the Flint family.

Billy and Tosher sat opposite each other in stony silence. Tosher made for a strange companion. Without the wig and veil, he looked like a rugby player whose little sister had been using his face to practise her make-up skills. Not a pretty sight.

"Long time no see," said Billy.

"Too soon for me," grunted Tosher. "My mum always said that you were a bad 'un."

"Oh yes," said Billy. "I'm terrible me. Fancy going

to church on a Sunday and joining the police! I'm a real embarrassment, aren't I?"

Tosher shrugged. "You always did think you were better than the rest of us."

"That's not hard when most of your family is in the nick and the rest are busy trying to get themselves sent there." Billy sighed. "I guess that's why you and your boys have left London, Tosher. On the run from the law again?"

"This is a legitimate business," said Tosher. "I ain't done nothin' wrong."

"Mmmm," said Billy doubtfully. "So your beauty treatments really work this time, do they?"

Tosher held his tongue.

"You mean they're not like the 'Arabian' beauty treatments that you were selling in London when you called yourself 'Madame Rachel'?" Billy got up and looked at the jars and bottles on the shelves. He picked up one labelled *Nile River Elixir*. "How much do you charge for this?"

"Five pounds," said Tosher.

Billy whistled softly between his teeth. "Not cheap, is it?"

"These old girls can all afford it."

129

"And it comes from the Nile, does it? I mean, it's not just water with a bit of sand in it?"

Tosher said nothing.

"And your other beauty treatments," Billy continued, "they are all *genuine* cosmetics, aren't they? Not powders and pastes that you mix up yourself from arsenic, lead powder, carbolic soap and prussic acid like last time?"

"They remove wrinkles," said Tosher defensively.

"They burn off *skin*," said Billy. "That's not really the same thing."

Tosher at least had the decency to look embarrassed. "What do want, Billy?" he said.

"I need information," said Billy. "I want the whispers from Edinburgh's criminal underground. And you're going to tell me everything I want to know…or I'm going straight to Inspector Diggins."

"What about family honour?" said Tosher.

"What *about* family honour? *I'm* the copper, *you're* the robber."

"Yeah, but you wouldn't tell on one of your own, would you?"

"Ask me again when we've finished this little chat," said Billy. "Oh, and one more thing – no more acid in your remedies. Buy some real treatments and flog *them* at outrageous prices if you must."

Tosher shrugged his broad shoulders and reached down the front of his dress. He pulled out an apple, leaving his chest oddly lopsided. He took a bite. "Want one?" he asked. "I've got a spare."

"I'll pass," said Billy. "Right, first up, what do you know about these jewellery robberies? Is there a housebreaking gang in Edinburgh? Have the jewels come up on the black market?"

Tosher took another bite of his apple. "Don't know what you're talking about."

"Really?" said Billy, stretching forward and snatching an unusual bird's-claw kilt pin which was attached to Tosher's dress. "Because this little beauty is an exact match for one that was stolen from Lady Lavinia Fitzpatrick. So let me ask you again: what do you know about it, Tosher?"

"I got the kilt pin from Razor – he's the one you should be asking."

Razor Flint. Not a name that Billy had been expecting to hear. Billy bit his lip. Razor Flint was not a nice man. "Where can I find him?" he said.

CHAPTER SEVENTEEN

MAC THE KNIFE

Every city has its forbidden streets. The dark alleys where terrible crimes are plotted by terrible people. That was where Billy went to meet Razor.

Tosher said that Razor could usually be found at the White Hart Inn. Billy could tell at a glance that the place was a den of thieves. He was sensitive to the stirrings of the spirit world but he knew that professional criminals were just as sensitive to the presence of a police officer. Before he went inside he turned up his collar and pulled a red scarf from his pocket, tying it loosely at his neck. It was the sort of scarf that "scuttlers" wore. A "scuttler" was a member of a ferocious street gang. It wasn't his best disguise, but it would have to do.

Setting his mouth in a vicious sneer to complete the street-gang look, Billy walked over to the bar. "I'm looking for Razor," he growled. "I've got a job for 'im."

"You won't find him here, pal," said the barman.

Billy took his penknife out and began to pick at his fingernails in what he hoped was a menacing way. "Try again," he said.

"Razor's left town," said the barman. With a twitch of his head, he indicated a table in the corner. "You could try askin' Mac the Knife, he did some business with Razor."

Billy looked over. Everything about Mac the Knife was big. Big hands for hitting. Big shoulders for carrying stolen goods. Big scar across his face. Presumably a big knife somewhere.

Billy strolled over and sat down opposite him, keeping up his own hard-man act. "I'm Billy Flint," he said, letting the criminal reputation of his family talk for him. "I'm after my cousin, Razor."

"He's gone away," grunted Mac. "Got scared."

Billy frowned. It would take something very scary to frighten cousin Razor. "Scared of what?"

"I can tell you," said Mac, "on account of you being family." The big man leaned forward to share his secret. "Razor gets things for people, right."

"Steals to order, you mean."

"Yeah, well, he had this client."

"A client who paid him with a very expensive gold bird's-claw kilt pin," said Billy.

Mac nodded. "Anyway, this client was strange, called himself the Sandman, and he wanted some very *unusual* things."

"Go on."

"Razor wanted me to help him get them," said Mac. "He had this list."

"Do you remember what was on it?"

"I'm not likely to forget," said Mac. "Milk from a black cow; the paw of a white cat; a mandrake root; the coins from a dead man's purse; a phoenix egg – whatever the heck that is – and…" Mac swallowed hard. "A fresh human heart."

Billy was stunned. "Did you get them all?"

"All but two," said Mac. "The egg…and the heart."

CHAPTER EIGHTEEN

The Ghost of a Chance

"What happened to you?" asked Charley as Billy pushed his way through the indoor jungle and into the crime lab. "You look as though you've seen a ghost."

"*Seen a ghost*," squawked Queen Victoria from somewhere in the tree canopy.

"Of course I have," he said. "We're S.C.R.E.A.M. It's in the job description."

"You know what I mean," said Charley. "Has something happened?"

Billy ran his hands through his hair. "This case gets

worse and worse... It'll end in murder if we can't stop it." He told her about the list.

"A phoenix egg?" said Charley. "That's got to be impossible to find."

"It's the human heart I'm worried about."

Charley rubbed her back with both hands, trying to ease the pain. "And did you get a name or a description of Razor's mysterious client?"

"Mac the Knife never met him, but he did have a name, or an alias anyway – the Sandman."

Charley gasped. "The warning note on the train was from the same person who is shopping for a heart."

"Exactly," said Billy. "Mac couldn't describe the Sandman, but Razor used to meet him at the Last Drop Tavern."

"The Last Drop Tavern?" said Doogie, appearing with a tray of sandwiches.

"Do you know it?" asked Billy.

"Oh aye," said Doogie. "The most haunted place in Edinburgh."

"Stands to reason," said Billy. "How about your investigation, Charley? What did you turn up?"

"Mrs Whisker, the housekeeper, was like the cat who got the cream," said Charley. "Lady Tiffin has gone to

London to recover from the shock of the burglary and it is clear that Mrs Whisker hasn't done a stroke of work since her mistress left." Charley smiled. "That worked to our advantage though – the lazy woman hadn't even tidied up the crime scene. She hadn't so much as swept up the sand…"

"More sand!"

"Yes," said Charley, "and there were more of those hieroglyphics that you found at Lady Fitzpatrick's. Including the two characters that were missing before!"

"So we've got the full message?"

"Oh yes," said Charley as she drew the symbols on the blackboard, the chalk squeaking. "At least I think so."

Billy looked at them. "A sort of bird and a block thingy? Do you know what they mean?"

"Not yet," said Charley. "I also need to find out what the Sandman wants those horrible ingredients for." She inhaled deeply. "I've got some reading to do." There was a mountain of leather-bound books in front of her. "The answers are in here somewhere."

"Right," said Billy. "That settles it. While Charley does the brain work, you and I are going to the pub, Doogie."

"What for?" asked Doogie. "Sir Gordon will be furious if he thinks I'm going for a drink."

"No drinking," said Billy, pulling on his coat. "We're looking for a different sort of spirit."

Doogie looked confused.

"A ghost."

"It's called the Last Drop because it's where all the hangings used to take place," said Doogie, as he and Billy rode together in the carriage, the zebras struggling in the wind and rain. 'Angry Annie' has haunted the tavern for years, so they say." The young lad was brimming over with enthusiasm. "I can't believe I'm solving crimes with a real policeman."

"You realize this is serious, don't you?" said Billy. "You haven't come along for a ride. You've got to be my backup."

Doogie's forehead furrowed.

"I'm going to try to make contact with a ghost," said Billy. "It's a stupidly dangerous thing to do. My life and soul are on the line, literally. So if I get into trouble, I'll need you to help me."

"How?"

"All police get issued with special equipment—"

"Like truncheons and handcuffs?"

"Sort of." Billy opened his satchel. "But S.C.R.E.A.M. detectives carry these."

Doogie peered inside the satchel with a confused expression. He pulled out a thorny stick. "You've got weeds in yer kit bag."

"That's hawthorn," Billy explained. "It can be used as protection from witchcraft. That one is garlic in case I meet a vampire, and that other plant is wolfsbane, which deters werewolves. I've got holy water in glass capsules, which I can fire using a catapult; I've got a crucifix to defend myself against demons and an iron box to trap sprites."

Doogie listened, enthralled. Or terrified. It was hard to say which.

"Anyway," said Billy, "this is what I've got for you."

"A bell, a book and a candle?" said Doogie with slight disappointment. Clearly he had been hoping for the catapult. "What am I supposed to do with these?"

"A ringing bell represents purity," said Billy. "It can

cast out certain unclean spirits. The book is a book of prayers, and the light of the candle can guide me home if I get...lost." Billy handed him the satchel. "Hopefully we won't need any of them."

The carriage halted outside the Last Drop Tavern. It was a dingy-looking building in the shadow of Edinburgh's great castle, on the same street as the White Hart Inn. Plucking up his courage, Billy led the way, running through the rain. Inside, he ordered two ginger beers from the barman and found a table next to the open fire. Billy put his hands towards the flames, enjoying the warmth.

The drinkers at the Last Drop certainly seemed to be a shady crowd. There were about twenty or so men, huddled in small shadowy groups beneath the low beams of the ceiling. The conversations were whispered, and when there was laughter it somehow sounded harsh and spiteful. Razor Flint would have been right at home.

"This is where my cousin Razor met the Sandman." Billy took a swig of his ginger beer. "Charley and I are convinced that the Sandman is the real villain we're up against, and he's using the mummy to do his dirty work. If this pub is haunted like you say, Doogie, then we might have found our perfect witness."

"How's that?"

"If Angry Annie is resident here then she will have seen *everything*, heard *everything*. As long as she's not 'Forgetful Annie' then we should be able to get a good description of the Sandman."

"Could ye not ask one of the living witnesses?" asked Doogie.

Billy cast his eyes around the room. "Which one of these gentlemen do you think would like to help the police with their enquiries?"

"Fair point," said Doogie, over the rim of his glass. "So how do ye think ye can get a ghost to tell ye what ye want?"

"I'm going to ask her nicely," said Billy. "And improvise."

"That means ye don't have a plan, doesn't it?"

Billy didn't get the chance to answer. A sudden gust of wind blew through the length of the pub. The candles and oil lamps spluttered, struggling to stay aflame. Doogie spun his head in the direction of the door, expecting to find a new customer standing there and letting in the draught. But the door was shut. There was no one there.

"I'm scared," said Doogie.

"Good," said Billy. "I'd be worried if you weren't."

The temperature inside the tavern began to fall. A deep unnatural coldness descended, far more bitter than the wind and rain outside. Doogie was shivering. He exhaled slowly, his breath misting the air. Then he placed his glass on the table, watching in horror as his ginger beer turned to ice.

Every conversation in the tavern stopped dead. They could all feel it; something bad was coming.

Billy saw the ghost girl standing in the darkest corner of the pub. She was small and frail, hardly more than a child. Billy wasn't an expert on historical costumes – that was much more Charley's field – but from the ruff around her neck and frills on her blouse, Billy knew that she had been haunting the Last Drop for a very long time.

Annie's hair was so fair that it looked like bleached bone. It floated around her face in long tendrils as if it had a life of its own. The ghost girl stared straight at Billy. Watching. Waiting. It was as if she had been there the whole time, playing hide-and-seek. But now Annie was bored with that game.

"Can you see her too?" asked Billy.

Doogie's eyes were screwed shut. "No," he said.

"*Before* you stopped looking?"

"Aye," said Doogie. "No…sort of. There was a glow, shaped like a wee girl."

Billy patted Doogie's arm. "You're doing well, Doogie. Stay strong for me."

Billy smiled gently at the ghost girl. "I'm your friend," he said warmly. Waves of emotion shot back at Billy, hitting him like a slap in the face. *Resentment. Shame… Sadness as deep and dark as the ocean.*

The temperature continued to plummet. The candle flames dwindled and began to die, snuffing out, one by one. Even the flames in the fireplace started to splutter and fizzle. Abnormal darkness began to fill the Last Drop Tavern. A total blackness, with Angry Annie's ghostly glow as the only light.

The barman was the first to make a run for it, leaping over his counter with surprising agility for a fat man and stumbling out into the street, apron flapping. The other drinkers were only seconds behind him. The dark and stormy night was suddenly far more appealing than another instant of this freezing terror.

Angry Annie looked straight at Billy. "I can seeee youuu," she said in a girlish sing-song. The girl smiled at Billy and it was somehow the most terrifying thing that she could have done. The overwhelming sadness that Annie had been wearing like a cloak seemed to drop away to be replaced by spiteful glee. A new emotion struck Billy: *anger, as fierce and savage as a wolf.*

Annie flung out one hand in a sweeping motion and a dozen beer glasses hurled themselves to the floor. She swept her hand again and tables overturned; chairs threw themselves against the walls and splintered to pieces. Although she was tiny, probably no more than eight or nine years old when she died, this wraithlike girl possessed incredible power. This was bad. Very bad. Annie might be the most powerful ghost Billy had ever encountered. He cursed himself for coming to the tavern so unprepared. It had been a mistake to let Doogie come with him too. Charley was trained to handle this sort of situation, but Doogie was just a lad and Billy shouldn't have dragged him into this.

And just when Billy was hoping the situation couldn't get any worse, Angry Annie started to scream. She flew across the room in a blur of white, stopping in front of him, her face so close to his that they were nearly touching. Her eyes were huge pools of blackness in her small white face. "Get out!" she snarled, her top lip curled back like an animal. "Leave me alone."

Billy didn't move. "Hello, Annabel," he said softly. Nothing in his voice betrayed the panic he felt inside. "My name is Billy and this is my friend, Doogie. I'd love to talk to you."

"Well, I don't want to talk to *you*!" Angry Annie shrieked. She gripped the table and threw it up into the air, smashing it like matchwood. Billy and Doogie fell back. Angry Annie reached for Billy with her spectral fingers. The tips touched his chest and then – terribly – pushed *through* Billy's clothes, his skin, his bone. Billy's whole body began to tremble uncontrollably as the ghostly hand wrapped around his heart, freezing him to death from the inside out.

CHAPTER NINETEEN

DEAD COLD

Doogie was petrified. The candles had all gone out and the only light was the ghost-glow. Doogie could see the outline of a wee girl shining through the darkness. Billy's hands were scrabbling at her, but passing through thin air. Doogie watched in horror as Billy's skin turned deathly white and the veins began to show through his flesh, thin lines of black creeping up from beneath his shirt collar.

Doogie didn't know what to do or how to help Billy. He had to do *something*, but how did you fight something that wasn't there? Doogie grabbed a bar stool from where it had fallen and threw it at the ghostly glow. The stool sailed right through and shattered on the floor. *Not like that then.*

Billy's entire body was shaking and Doogie could see ice crystallizing around his nostrils and across his eyelashes. The detective opened his mouth as if to scream, but the inside of his mouth was frozen too – tongue, cheeks, lips – everything that was soft and wet inside Billy's mouth was covered with jagged spikes of ice.

That awful sight snapped Doogie back to his senses and he remembered the bag that Billy had given him. He pulled out the bell. He gave it a vigorous shake. No sound came. Doogie shook it again and then realized that the brass clapper was frozen to the inside of the bell! Doogie banged the bell on the table, trying to jolt the clapper free.

Billy's back arched and long icicles began to erupt from his body, like the spines of a hedgehog…

Time was running out; Doogie smashed the bell down, turning his fear into brute strength – and the clapper broke loose! With a sense of triumph, Doogie rang the bell for all he was worth. It made a beautiful sound, although he couldn't understand how it could be a weapon. He rang it again, louder and harder.

Somehow it did the trick. The ice started to thaw, the icicles shrunk.

"The book," Billy gasped. "Open it, then slam it shut."

That made even less sense, but Doogie did as he was told. He took out the prayer book, opened it at the middle, and then snapped it shut as hard as he could. It closed with a *bang!* as solid and heavy as a prison door being slammed. Doogie could feel the vibrations it sent out and when the sound hit Billy, the effect was instantaneous. The last of the icicles which had impaled the detective melted away and Billy slumped to the floor.

Doogie ran to his side; Billy was unconscious and as cold as stone. Quickly, Doogie thought of what Mr Cowley would do – and he slapped Billy hard across the cheek.

Billy groaned but remained unconscious. Doogie was about to slap him again when he remembered the third piece of emergency equipment – *a candle, to guide me back.*

The blue glimmering of the ghost girl had retreated to the corner of the tavern, but it was still there, flitting back and forth. Was Angry Annie preparing to strike again? With shaking fingers, Doogie got out the candle and fumbled to light a match… *But what if Angry Annie blows it out?* Doogie rang the bell again, and it seemed to keep the ghost at bay…for now.

With the candle lit, Doogie brought it close to Billy's face. "Come back," he said. *"Please!"*

Billy started to cough; then his eyes fluttered open.

"Well done, mate," said Billy, struggling into a sitting position. "I owe you one."

"Ye mean like a reward?" said Doogie, beaming.

"I was thinking more like my deepest thanks," said Billy.

"Oh," said Doogie, trying to keep the disappointment from his voice. "That's nice too."

"Right," said Billy, all business again. He took the candle in one hand and the bell in the other. "You stay ready with that book, Doogie. I'm going to try again."

Doogie saw the ghost-glow spin frantically, like a bird trapped in a cage hurling itself against the bars in an attempt to get free.

"Are all the English as mad as ye?"

CHAPTER TWENTY

INTERVIEW WITH A GHOST

That had been close. Angry Annie lived up to her name and Billy now knew that she was able to channel all of that pent-up fury into devastating power. He wouldn't tell Charley that he had nearly died; she'd be ever so cross with him.

However, now that Annie had been restrained by the combined effect of the bell, book and candle, Billy had to try to get through to her again. This was not just about *his* life. The Sandman was after a human heart – he had to be stopped.

Billy picked up a stool that hadn't been broken and set

it upright at a table, as casually as if he were meeting an old friend for a chat and a laugh. He kept his eyes fixed on Angry Annie the whole time. The ghost was pacing back and forth like a caged tiger, wary of the power of the bell, book and candle – but not tamed, not safe.

Billy held up the bell for Annie to see. The ghost flinched back, fearing that it would be rung again. "Look," said Billy, quietly and calmly, "I'm putting down the bell. I'm sorry that we had to use it." Doogie shifted uncomfortably, obviously less convinced that Angry Annie could be reasoned with.

"Let's start again, shall we?" Billy continued. "My name is Billy. I've not come here to hurt you…" Inside, Billy's stomach was churning as if he had swallowed a live eel – Annie had nearly frozen the blood in his veins! But outside, he was as calm as a millpond, not a ripple of fear showing on the surface. Annie floated closer…

"I need your help, Annie," said Billy.

Annie's black eyes flared. "Why should I help you?" she snarled.

"I can't *make* you help me," said Billy honestly. "But *I* can help *you*."

"You can't do anything for me!" shouted Annie, her anger building again.

"I can set you free," said Billy quietly. "You've been here for such a long time, wouldn't you like to go... home?"

That small, simple word had a powerful effect on the ghost girl. It was as if it was Annie's turn to freeze. She said nothing. Her black eyes were unreadable. She didn't move at all and after the constant restless movement, the ghost's sudden stillness scared Billy. What would Angry Annie do now?

"Home?" she repeated slowly. "You mean that I could be free from all this?" Her eyes darted furiously around the Last Drop Tavern, her prison for hundreds of years.

Billy nodded. "Would you like that, Annie? Would you like to be at peace?"

"Peace?" Annie's lips curled back like a dog about to bark, showing her small sharp teeth. Billy took a step back, ready to grab the bell again if Annie went for him.

But she didn't.

Billy sensed the air begin to warm ever-so-softly, as if Annie's endless anger was beginning to thaw.

"Could you really do that?" she breathed.

Billy nodded again. "It would be my pleasure," he said. In that instant Billy saw Annie as if he was seeing her for the first time; not as a vicious wraith but a little girl. A girl who was lost and so very alone. His heart went out to her…even if she had just tried to murder him.

"And if I don't help you? Are you going to make me stay here for ever? Punish me more?" The temperature started to drop again.

"No," said Billy, quite calm. "I'm still going to set you free, whether you help me or not. I promise."

"Why?"

"Because it's the right thing to do."

"But you don't know me. You don't know what I did." Annie's voice was filled with remorse.

"I don't need to know. I'm sure that whatever it was, it was a long time ago and I can see from your eyes that you're sorry now—"

"More than anything," said Annie, fat tears rolling down her face and freezing on her cheeks like diamonds. "Billy, how can I help you?"

"There is a man – an *evil* man, who calls himself the Sandman – and he has to be stopped, Annie. I need a description if I'm to have any chance of tracking him down."

"I know the Sandman," said Annie. "I've heard his whispered plans, his monstrous desires."

CHAPTER TWENTY-ONE

HOT WATER

Billy had left the tavern with a description of the Sandman, and the repeated promise to Annie that he would return to keep his half of the bargain.

He ran through Annie's words over and over, trying to picture the Sandman clearly. *Cold and hard, like a rock. Chiselled features, nose like a hawk. Tall. Lean. Dark eyes. Very controlled, precise in his movements. Smartly dressed in a black suit. Not a hair out of place. And he carries a wand made out of bone.*

The description reminded Billy of someone but he couldn't quite place who. It would come to him. For now

Billy was exhausted. So tired he could hardly walk, so drained he couldn't think straight. Although he and Annie had parted as friends, her ghostly touch had been so cold, Billy wondered if he would ever feel warm again.

The day was fading and Billy shivered all the way back to 44 Morningside Place. Doogie didn't say a word, but as soon as the carriage arrived he jumped out and ran on ahead. "I'll get Beth to run a bath for you," he called back. "It might take some of that chill off."

Following slowly after Doogie, Billy entered the great house. Wellington was waiting in the hallway, his claws clicking on the polished tiles. The dog seemed jumpy, but he was pleased to see Billy and came scampering over. "I feel it too," whispered Billy, scratching behind Wellington's ears. "You live in a strange house, don't you, boy?"

Just then, a sharp trace of supernatural energy hit Billy in the nostrils. It rocked him back on his heels and made his eyes sting as if he had stuck his nose in a mustard jar and had a good sniff. Billy wobbled and flung out a hand to save himself from falling over, almost knocking a plant from its pedestal.

"Are you all right?" said Charley, coming to greet him. "What is it?"

"I don't know," said Billy honestly, the dizziness passing as quickly as it had come. "This house, this case." He gave a shrug. "It's gone now, anyway."

"Wellington has been going mad for the last half-hour or so," said Charley.

"We both know that animals can be more in tune with the spirit realm than humans sometimes," said Billy.

"Back at the railway station, it was Wellington who noticed something lurking before any of us," said Charley. The Scottish terrier had stopped pacing and was curled up in his basket by the door. "He seems happy enough now though."

"Like I said," said Billy, "it was probably nothing. I'm fine." He slapped his legs to demonstrate their sturdiness.

"How did your investigation go?"

"I've got a description of the Sandman. I've written it all in my notebook," said Billy, handing it over. "How about you?"

"I'm close to cracking those hieroglyphs, I think," said Charley. "Get warmed up and then we can compare notes."

Charley set off for the crime lab and Billy climbed the stairs to the bathroom. When he'd been growing up the only bath he knew was a tin one that his mother put out in the kitchen and filled with kettles of water from the stove. The bathroom at 44 Morningside Place was not like that.

Billy opened the door and was immediately enfolded in a warm cloud of steam. The air smelled of lavender and soap. Tiny bubbles floated all around. Billy walked over to the bathtub. It was filled almost to the brim and Beth had used bath salts which turned the water cloudy but would ease away all the frost that still clung to his bones.

Billy quickly undressed and then lowered himself into the hot water. A wave of dizziness came over him again, but quickly passed. He dismissed it as a combination of tiredness and the heat of the water – almost too hot, but not quite. Billy let his head fall back and slid in up to his shoulders. He was suddenly so relaxed, he could almost fall asleep right here, wrapped up in this blanket of warmth and bubbles. *Heaven.*

Something rough bumped against the inside of his calf. Beth must have put in a sponge or a loofah. Very kind of her. Billy smiled. He could get used to this.

His shoulders really did ache and he couldn't wait to give them a good scrub. The loofah had floated further up the bath now; it was touching his thigh. It really was very rough as sponges went. Still, all the better to rub away every trace of the Last Drop Tavern. Too tired to even look at what he was doing, Billy groped blindly in the water.

And the sponge bit him!

At least that was what it felt like. Billy whipped his hand away and sat up to examine his stinging fingers. Sure enough, there was a trace of blood. *What the…?*

He peered through the haze of steam, trying to make out what had been sharp enough in the bath to slice through his skin. Billy could see the long, thin shape of the loofah. It was scaly, it was moving, and it had a mouthful of jagged teeth.

Billy froze for a second before he realized what it was – the mummified baby crocodile! Only it wasn't in Sir Gordon's Egyptian hall any more. It was in Billy's bath, and it was very much alive. Between Billy's legs. And its jaws were opening wide!

CHAPTER TWENTY-TWO

HOUSE OF HORRORS

Billy shot up in the air just as those horrible jaws snapped shut.

He winced as he thought of what he could have lost. He tried to scramble to his feet, but the bath was so slippery that he slid down, giving the monster a second chance. His head went under the surface, sending water sloshing everywhere, and when he came back up again, gasping, he was face-to-face with the bizarre crocodile mummy. Billy noticed that someone had cut the bandages along its scaly mouth, freeing up those savage jaws. Free to make a meal out of him!

Snap! Snap! Snap! The jaws crunched together again and again and Billy struggled backwards, clinging to the sides of the bathtub for dear life while his feet struggled to get a grip on the soapy enamel. The mummy's bandages were falling apart now in the hot water, revealing more of the undead reptile inside. The leathery hide had turned from green to brown, and the eye sockets were empty, giving Billy a view of the hollow skull inside. Somehow Billy managed to half fall, half throw himself out and tumbled to the bathroom floor in a naked heap.

His heart pounding wildly, Billy looked around for something – *anything* – he could use for protection. Billy had hoped that the crocodile mummy would stay in the water and enjoy a little swim. But one look at those scrabbling dead claws told Billy that he wouldn't be so lucky. The crocodile hadn't eaten for thousands of years and had woken up hungry! Although it only had short stubby legs, it clearly had an enormously powerful tail of mummified flesh and to Billy's horror it used all that brute force to hurl itself over the edge of the bath.

Billy backed away into the corner of the bathroom while the crocodile mummy scurried across the floor towards him, tail flicking. In desperation Billy put his fingers behind the bathroom cabinet, a tall and ugly piece of furniture laden with bottles of medicine and lotions. The cabinet was incredibly heavy but the fear of being eaten alive was just the sort of motivation that Billy needed to summon up enough strength to send it toppling over.

It fell like an oak tree, smashing down on the crocodile mummy and showering it with a thousand pieces of broken glass, which covered the bathroom floor like lethal confetti. On top of that, the cabinet had also fallen across the door, blocking his only escape. The window was tiny, and even if he could slip through, the bathroom was on the second floor – the drop could kill him. The crocodile mummy was stunned but not defeated. Its tail continued to twitch and Billy could hear its claws ripping at the floor as it tried to free itself.

Billy looked at his bare feet and the broken glass. He snatched his shirt off the floor where he had dropped it and quickly ripped it in two, then wrapped it round his feet. It wasn't much protection, but it would have to do. Meanwhile the crocodile was almost free. Running out of options, Billy grabbed the largest towel that he could find. Holding it up like a bullfighter with a red flag, Billy advanced on the crocodile, just as it broke loose with a final swipe of its tail.

The crocodile seemed to be preparing itself for another assault, but Billy knew that he had to act first. Before the animal was able to leap at him, Billy threw himself down on top of it with the towel spread wide. The creature was caught by surprise. Billy could feel its raw strength – a *supernatural* strength – rippling through its long-dead muscles. It was only now, up this close to the crocodile, that Billy could sense the aura of magick that had been used to animate it.

All this time Billy had thought that 44 Morningside Place was so cluttered with bizarre objects that his sixth sense was clouded out, but now he wondered whether it had been blocked deliberately. He could worry about that later though. He had an undead crocodile to deal with now. Still lying flat on top of the creature while it bucked and thrashed beneath him, Billy did his best to work the towel underneath it. The idea – and it wasn't one of his best – was to wrap the crocodile in the towel. If he could do it quickly and as tightly as possible then it should be enough to restrain the beast. At the very least he hoped to be able to wrap up those savage jaws.

He knew that working for S.C.R.E.A.M. was a dangerous job, but he'd never imagined that it might end like this: attacked by an undead crocodile; naked and armed only with a towel. What would Charley say?

"Blast!" said Charley. "Damn and blast with shiny knobs on!"

S.C.R.E.A.M. was at the cutting edge of modern policing. The methodical approach which Luther Sparkwell had taught them, the minute examination of crime scenes for traces which might identify a perpetrator or reveal vital clues as to their whereabouts, the groundbreaking use of science as an instrument of detection – not to mention Billy's special spiritual gift – all these were streets ahead of most local police work.

So with all these modern advances at her disposal, Charley found it especially annoying that at that precise moment her investigation was being hampered by an interfering parrot.

There she was, working her way through a mountain of reference books and trying to work out what the Sandman's grotesque shopping list was for, when Queen Victoria had swooped down from the branches above and snatched Charley's silver fountain pen out of her hand. And now the dratted bird was sitting overhead and laughing at her.

"*God save me! God save me!*" Queen Victoria squawked, her head bobbing up and down. "*We are not amused!*"

"I'm not amused either," muttered Charley. For about the hundredth time that day she hated being in a wheelchair. Charley made a point of never complaining, never making a fuss, but, honestly, it would be so much easier if she could walk. Queen Victoria had stashed her pen in the crook of a branch – if Charley could climb she would have got it back in seconds. But of course, she couldn't climb. Normally she wouldn't have been bothered about a stupid old pen, but it was her favourite one, with a personal inscription from the Prime Minister after S.C.R.E.A.M. had sorted out a little problem with an actual skeleton in his cupboard. So here she was, searching around for something to throw at the pen in the hope of dislodging it.

There were stones around the ornamental fountain and she took one of those, hefting it in her hand for weight. Charley took careful aim, threw it…and missed. Her missile sailed over the branch, clean past Queen Victoria – and straight through the glass wall of the conservatory with a jangling crash.

With a sense of resignation, Charley wheeled around the trees to inspect the damage she had done.

Sir Gordon's indoor jungle was impressive during the day, but at night it had a different atmosphere. The leaves that were such brilliant greens in the sunlight were now all black, and they crowded around Charley, making her feel trapped. There was a stirring in the undergrowth and she stopped dead in her tracks. It sounded as if she was not alone.

Charley tensed, straining her ears to hear. The noise came again: a definite rustle of leaves, followed by the soft padding of feet. Queen Victoria was somewhere above her. Prince Albert, the massive snake, was coiled sleepily around a tree. The spiders and scorpions were in their glass tank, feasting on dead mice. Something else was coming her way.

The footsteps got closer. And closer.

Charley felt sure that only a curtain of leaves separated her from the other presence in the lab. "Billy Flint," she said, grabbing the branches and pulling them apart. "I'm really not in the mood for your silly—"

A face stared back at her from between the branches – but it wasn't Billy's. This was a nightmare face, with two holes where eyes had once been. The ragged bandages couldn't disguise a long, flat, ape-like skull, with flaring nostrils on the end of an elongated snout. Clumps of wiry hair emerged through the gaps in the rotting cloth. *It was the mummified baboon!*

The baboon screeched in Charley's face, its grave breath making her skin creep. As quickly as she could, Charley wheeled backwards out of its reach towards her workbench.

The baboon ran up a tree into the canopy of leaves overhead. Charley was shocked to see a flash of its bum, still bright red after thousands of years, mooning out from the tatters of its bandages. The baboon was quicker than her, and most likely stronger too. Charley knew she couldn't match this beast in a physical fight, but she firmly believed that science could find a way where brute force wouldn't. Providing she could make it to the chemistry set alive...

"What is it, boy?" said Doogie.

Doogie had taken Wellington for his evening walk but the little terrier had been skittish ever since they returned to 44 Morningside Place. They were standing together in the entrance hall and Wellington was barking furiously.

The hair stood up across the dog's shoulders as he growled at something only he could see.

Doogie crouched down to the dog's level. "What is it, laddie?" The dog's lips curled back in a snarl and Doogie did his best to follow Wellington's line of sight.

That was when Doogie saw it too. It looked like a cat.

"How did that get in?" Doogie wondered. He was about to shoo the thing back out onto the street when he saw what sort of cat it was.

A dead cat. Wrapped in mouldy bandages, prowling through the house as if it owned the place.

The mummified cat hissed at Wellington, its skeletal tail twitched and then it took off like a flash, with the plucky terrier in pursuit. The chase was on! Doogie watched in horror as the animals unleashed mayhem in Sir Gordon's house, hissing and growling, spitting and barking.

War was declared, and it was the cat that made the first strike. Needle-sharp claws emerged from its bandaged paws as it suddenly ran forward and took a swipe at Wellington's nose, drawing blood. Wellington howled in pain and outrage, and then shot towards the cat, determined to get his own back. The cat leaped from the floor and used its claws to climb up an expensive tapestry. Then it perched calmly near the top; gloating as only cats can. Wellington grabbed the edge of the tapestry in his teeth, and pulled as hard as he could.

"No, Wellington!" yelled Doogie. "Bad doggy."

Wellington didn't care.

The tapestry tumbled to the ground, bringing the cat with it.

The mummy landed on its feet, then arched its back, its ancient spine making horrible crunching noises, tail straight up in the air. It circled the terrier, looking for its moment to pounce. Wellington glared back from underneath his massive eyebrows, nostrils flaring, hair bristling. The dog drew back his lip to show his teeth… and the cat mummy retreated. In a graceful fluid movement, it leaped over Wellington's bemused head and on to one of Sir Gordon's display cabinets.

Doogie's hands went to his mouth in horror as first one, then two, then three of His Lordship's treasures came crashing to the floor. "Oh jings!" Doogie cursed, rushing over and trying to catch the next ornament to be sent tumbling as the mummy cat ran along the top of the cabinets, leaving destruction in its wake. Doogie made a diving leap and got his hands around a crystal vase just in time… Although he was still one step behind the cat, which had jumped over to balance on the shoulder of one of Sir Gordon's Greek statues.

The smug cat sat on the marble woman's shoulder and seemed very happy there. Or at least it was until Wellington ran at the narrow plinth on which the statue was balanced and threw his paws against it with full force. The cat mummy jumped clear, a strip of bandage flapping after it it like an extra tail. The statue wobbled... then fell, landing against another statue which also fell, this time into a priceless Ming vase.

Wellington's black hair was powdered with white dust from the smashed statues. He gave a doggy sneeze and then looked around again for his arch-enemy. The mummy cat was slinking off towards the crime lab. Wellington set off in hot pursuit.

Doogie ran after them, muttering.

"This isn't gonna end well!"

Charley made it to the workbench first – but only just. The baboon mummy jumped down out of the trees and landed on the table with a crash, rattling the glass bottles.

It was a monstrous creature, Charley thought. The human mummy had been bad but there was something especially terrifying about this undead ape. Even in life the only intelligence which the baboon had possessed was pure animal cunning: kill, eat, repeat. Charley didn't know whether this rotting monster would actually eat her, but she didn't doubt that it could rip her to shreds. It screamed again, its mouth opening so wide that the ancient flesh at the corners of its lips was ripping with the strain.

Charley's eye scanned the bottles of chemicals in front of her until she found the one that she was after – sulphuric acid. That should slow it down! She pulled the glass stopper from the bottle at the same instant that the baboon took a swing at her. The ape's mighty fist sent the chemicals on the workbench flying, and Charley was grateful for the blanket across her legs as a deadly acid rain fell all around, scorching everything it touched.

Charley threw the whole bottle of acid at the baboon's legs and then wheeled backwards with every ounce of strength she possessed.

The effect was extraordinary, from a scientific point of view. In every other respect it was ghastly.

When the concentrated acid struck the animal's legs there was a mighty hissing roar – and the monster began to dissolve. Plumes of smoke rose from the creature as the lower half of its body began to liquefy. The baboon's legs collapsed into a bubbling mess, a revolting soup of bandages, bones and ancient flesh until only the upper half remained, twitching in the pool that used to be its body.

Charley let out a sigh of relief.

The baboon snorted with anger and then started to crawl towards her, dragging its stumps behind it.

CHAPTER TWENTY-THREE

THE SANDS OF TIME

Charley met Doogie running into the crime lab as she was propelling herself out. Two shapes rushed past her: a dead cat being chased by a terrier who was very much alive.

"This way!" said Charley, grabbing Doogie's arm and dragging him away from the lab.

Doogie glanced over Charley's shoulder and spotted the mummy baboon, crawling towards them, teeth bared. "Where are we going?"

"To the lift," said Charley.

If she couldn't stop the baboon then Charley at least

wanted to prevent the thing from reaching her. They arrived at the lift, and after some wasted moments fumbling with the mechanism, the metal gates opened wide. "Inside, quick!" said Charley, shoving Doogie in and following after, slamming the doors shut behind her. Charley was locking them again when a pair of leathery hands, partially wrapped in decaying bandage, grabbed the cage from the outside.

The baboon began to shake the bars, screaming and screeching. Charley hadn't been able to secure the locking mechanism, but she didn't dare come within the baboon's reach. Experimentally she inched forwards and the baboon responded by shoving its snout between the bars, snapping savagely. Then it pushed its arm through too, swiping at Charley, forcing her to back away.

She knew that there was no brain in its head, no air in its lungs...actually no lungs at all... And yet there was a magical fire that burned inside the beast, driving its withered muscles and crumbling bones to attack.

And then, quite suddenly, that mystic fire went out. The arm fell limp. The mouth hung open.

Cautiously, Charley poked the mummy; it didn't respond.

With a creak and a jerk, the lift sprang into action,

carrying Doogie and Charley up to the first floor. The baboon came with them, its stiff arm still stuck between the bars. Billy was waiting for them upstairs.

"I see you've dressed for the occasion," said Charley, taking in the towel that was wrapped around his midriff. "What have you got there?" she asked, pointing to the long object he was carrying, bundled in another towel.

With a flourish, Billy let the towel slip and the baby crocodile rolled out. It hit the floor with a heavy thwack, as lifeless as a plank of wood. "It was attacking me," said Billy.

"And then it stopped," Charley finished. "Any idea why?"

"Just a theory," said Billy. "I think that they were being controlled by someone and for whatever reason the connection broke."

"Like cutting a puppet's strings?" suggested Doogie.

"Exactly," said Billy. "But who is the puppetmaster?"

"Someone who wants us dead," said Charley softly.

Five minutes later Billy was dressed again and back in the crime lab with Charley. They had locked the crocodile and the baboon inside the lift cage, just in case the

Sandman woke them up for a second round. Wellington, meanwhile, was digging a hole beneath one of the trees and burying something. It looked suspiciously like a mummified cat.

"The Sandman is even more powerful than we imagined," said Billy. "I think he even has the power to cloak his abilities and stay hidden from me."

"And I think I know what his goal is," said Charley. "I knew I remembered the Sandman's list from somewhere. I've been rummaging through Sir Gordon's library. Listen to this." She picked up a tattered book and began to read. "This is from the diary of John Dee, magician in the court of Queen Elizabeth I." Charley cleared her throat. "Root of a mandrake, paw of a white cat, milk from a black cow, coins from a dead man's purse, the sparkling phoenix egg, a human heart... Sound familiar?

"Well, according to John Dee, the Sandman is gathering everything he needs to become immortal."

Billy was stunned. "So out there somewhere is a man with enough knowledge of Egyptian magick to reanimate mummies, with a fortune in stolen jewels to buy whatever he wants, and the dream of living for ever... It's incredible."

"It's terrible," said Charley.

"At least we've got a reliable description of him now," said Billy. "That's something to go on."

"But not enough!" said Charley.

Billy continued pacing. "What about the burglaries? What linked them?"

"The victims were guests of Sir Gordon," said Charley. "Very wealthy, obviously."

"And on each occasion the mummy knew exactly where to look, which suggests that no matter how powerful a magician the Sandman is, he is being given information by someone on the inside."

"The other thing that links the burglaries is the traces of Saharan sand," said Charley.

"The circles with the hieroglyphics," said Billy. "You've translated them, haven't you, Duchess?"

"I've got a *partial* translation," said Charley, with frustration. She wheeled over to her blackboard. "We got four glyphs at Lady Fitzpatrick's and two more at Lady Tiffin's, and combined they give us this sequence. The trouble is that because they are written in a circle, I can't know for certain which glyph is the start of the sentence."

Sir Gordon joined them then, announcing his arrival in the crime lab with a polite cough. "Thought I'd come and see how you two detectives are getting on," he said quietly. "Don't like being on my own in the house right now, what with most of the servants gone, and the living dead on the rampage destroying everything I own." He sounded pitiful but he brightened a little when he looked at the blackboard. "Hieroglyphics, eh?"

"You must understand a lot of it yourself," said Charley, talking to the man over her shoulder, "having excavated a genuine Egyptian tomb."

"Well," said Sir Gordon, "I haven't done much actual studying myself… So, let me see if I've got this right? The funny little pictures are words?"

"Yes," said Charley as patiently as she could manage. "The funny little pictures are words."

"So what does it say?"

Charley furrowed her brow. "To make – or possibly see – a servant fly in an instant *something* power."

"I don't get it," said Sir Gordon.

"Neither do I," said Charley, "and it isn't helped by the fact that I haven't been able to find a meaning for one of the glyphs at all." She circled one of the hieroglyphs with such force that she snapped her chalk in half.

"The Sandman has been one step ahead of us the whole time," said Billy. "We know what he wants but we don't know how to stop him."

"Ah, yes, you told me about this Sandman chappy. Sounds like an absolute scoundrel," said Sir Gordon. "What exactly does he want?"

Billy shared a look with Charley. Sir Gordon was hardly going to be able to help, was he? "The only things the Sandman still needs are a phoenix egg and a human heart."

"Oh," said Sir Gordon. "I know a fellow who's got a phoenix egg."

"What?" spluttered Billy.

"It's a beautiful thing," said Sir Gordon. "A really massive ruby, must have cost a fortune. It's so big that it's called the 'Phoenix Egg'."

"Who has it?" said Charley.

"Lord Martin Wintersfall," said Sir Gordon. "A good friend of mine – he thoroughly enjoyed my mummy party. Or at least he did until the mummy came to life and went on the rampage."

"Where does Lord Wintersfall live?"

"At The Grange, a magnificent house, about fifteen minutes from here by zebra."

"I'm going now!" said Billy, grabbing his jacket.

"You won't be able to stop the mummy from stealing the jewel, it's too strong, we know that," Charley warned.

"I don't plan to stop the mummy," said Billy. "If it comes for the Phoenix Egg, I'm going to follow it back to the Sandman's lair!"

CHAPTER TWENTY-FOUR

THE WRITING ON THE WALL

Although Billy had said that he wouldn't try to stop the mummy, it didn't hurt to go prepared. He had borrowed a cricket bat and Sir Gordon's new blunderbuss, in case things really cut up rough. Charley's bullets hadn't stopped the mummy, but the blunderbuss – with its massive barrel shaped like a trumpet – could blow a hole in just about anything. Backup was also coming; Doogie had been sent to summon Inspector Diggins and his men. Nine times out of ten the local police just got in the way of a S.C.R.E.A.M. investigation, but Billy wouldn't say no to having some more muscle to call on if he got into a confrontation with the Sandman and his bandage-wrapped sidekick. Best of all, Billy had plucky Wellington at his side.

It was still dark when Billy arrived at The Grange. It was the most impressive house he had seen yet, even putting 44 Morningside Place to shame. But there was something sinister and unwelcoming about it. It probably didn't help that it was situated next to a graveyard.

Billy and Wellington approached the front door and after a few minutes of banging they were greeted by the housekeeper, who was clearly annoyed to have been dragged out of bed.

"Tradesmen go round the back," she barked.

"Policemen walk right in," said Billy, flashing his badge.

"Begging your pardon," said the housekeeper. "I didn't realize you was an officer of the law."

"I'll let you off this time," said Billy, with a twinkle in his eyes. "I'm sorry it's the middle of the night, but I must speak to Lord Wintersfall."

"His Lordship is at Balmoral," said the housekeeper, "as a guest of Her Majesty. And the butler, Mr Humble, had some urgent personal business which has taken him away tonight. Can I help you?"

"I need two things," said Billy. "Firstly, I need to know where Lord Wintersfall keeps his jewels. I think that someone might try to steal them tonight."

The housekeeper's hand went to her mouth in shock. "And the second?"

"You couldn't rustle up some cheese and pickle, could you?" said Billy. "Fighting crime really takes it out of you."

Charley scribbled away on the blackboard while Sir Gordon watched, half dozing in a chair. She was determined to unravel the riddle of the hieroglyphics no matter how tired she felt. Her sleeves were covered in chalk dust up to the elbow. Charley tried a new combination of the glyphs, frowned at it, and then scrubbed it away. If only she could translate that last blasted symbol.

She gazed at it for the thousandth time. What was it meant to be? *A bowl? A plank?* Charley turned her head on its side. Could it possibly be…*a door?*

183

Working at lightning speed, Charley reordered the hieroglyphs, starting the sentence with a different character.

"I've got it!" she said, waking Sir Gordon with a start. "It reads, *The power to make my servant fly in an instant through the door.* Do you see what that means?!"

"Yes!" said Sir Gordon, then he paused. "Actually, no."

Charley was about to explain when they were interrupted by Doogie.

"Sorry to bother ye, Your Lordship, but I've found something... I'm afraid you're not gonna like it."

"What have you got there?" asked Charley.

Doogie was holding three small wooden objects in his hands. Boxes. Or tiny coffins. Gingerly, he placed them on the workbench.

"I found one in your room while I was cleaning, Your Lordship, and one in yours, Miss Charley, and one in Master Billy's," said Doogie. "They were hidden under your beds."

"And why were you doing a housemaid's job?" asked Sir Gordon.

"Beth's gone," said Doogie, "run away to somewhere the mummy can't get her. And Mrs Fudge has packed her bags and gone to stay at her sister's B&B – said she couldn't take it no more."

"Mr Cowley has gone too," said Sir Gordon on the verge of tears. "Handed in his notice this morning, said he was moving back in with his mother. Rats deserting the sinking ship."

"At least Doogie is loyal to you," said Charley.

"I don't have anywhere else to go," said Doogie with a shrug.

Charley ran her fingers through her long ginger hair and returned to the coffin-shaped boxes. She took a pair of tweezers and carefully eased their lids open. Part of her wished she hadn't.

Each one had a lumpen wax figure inside.

"Poppets," she said quietly.

"What?"

"Nasty things," said Charley. "Human figures used in witchcraft and sorcery."

Although the mannequins were crude, it was obvious who they were meant to be. One was fat, with a bright waistcoat button hidden inside its rounded belly, just visible through the wax. One was a boy, with a red scarf at his neck, and what appeared to be a scorpion sting protruding from its waxy flesh. The last one was thinner, more feminine, with strands of ginger hair plastered to the head. Looking closer, Charley saw that there was something within the chest cavity itself. She lifted the horrible wax doll out of its coffin and held it to her ear. She was right; there was a faint *tick-tick-tick*ing coming from inside.

Taking a scalpel, Charley carved through the grey wax to find a silver object buried there like a beating heart. "That's my watch," she said, relieved to have it back, but her stomach churned to find it like this.

There was another metal object inside the doll's head, just above the slit that was meant to be Charley's left eye. Using the tweezers again, she pulled it free. It was a pin.

The stabbing pain that had crippled Charley soon after she'd arrived at 44 Morningside Place suddenly made awful sense. Voodoo witch doctors used these sort of charms to control or hurt people, but the Egyptian magicians had done it first.

"There's a pin in your poppet too," said Charley, indicating the sliver of steel that pierced the stomach of the fat little wax figure. "That's how it works. The magician inflicts pain on the poppet and the victim feels it for real."

"That terrible agony." Sir Gordon placed his hand on his belly. "That was caused by the Sandman," he said.

Charley had been afraid. Now she was angry. "I've been so stupid!" She slammed her forehead with the palm of her hand. "The Sandman has been right under our noses all along!"

"This is all my fault!" Sir Gordon wailed. "I never meant to bring the curse down on us all."

"Don't despair," said Charley, seeing Sir Gordon sinking deeper into a hole of self-pity.

"Ach, but ye haven't seen this yet," said Doogie. He led them out of the crime lab to the hall, stopping in front of the portrait of Sir Gordon. "This is enough to put the wind up anyone's kilt."

The portrait had been vandalized in the most horrific and personal way. Sir Gordon's face had been slashed with a knife, leaving the canvas hanging in tattered ribbons. Then, in case that message was too subtle, the vandal had also painted on the portrait in dripping red paint:

REVENGE SHALL BE MINE

"All right," said Charley. "Now you can despair if you want to, but I haven't got time."

She spun her chair round and headed straight back to the lab. "I've got work to do."

CHAPTER TWENTY-FIVE

INTO THE WHIRLWIND

"Anything else you need?" asked the housekeeper.

Billy finished his bread and cheese and smacked his lips. At his feet, Wellington was tucking into a bowl of tripe. "Any biscuits going?" he asked.

Suddenly Billy felt overwhelmingly tired. He hadn't had a decent night's sleep since the case began, and the warmth of the fire and the comfort of the armchair were taking effect. Wellington curled up on a tiger-skin rug and started to snore. Lord Wintersfall's safe sat in the corner of the room, a huge squat box with the Phoenix Egg inside. The blunderbuss and the cricket bat were both within easy reach. Billy knew he should have asked for a coffee to go with those biscuits. Oh well, five minutes sleep wouldn't hurt anyone...

Billy was just beginning to nod when his sixth sense started to tingle, like spiders running around inside his head. He leaped up, totally alert. Danger was far better than caffeine at keeping him awake.

Something was wrong.

Billy felt a hot wetness on his top lip and instinctively touched it. His fingers came away red. Blood had started to pour from his nose as a wave of approaching magick overwhelmed him.

In his mind's eye, Billy was in an Egyptian temple. The Sandman was there, towering above him. The man's face was in shadow but Billy knew it had to be him; he was holding a curved bone wand in one hand...and a fresh human heart in the other! The Sandman was not alone – he was flanked by creatures that looked like gods...evil, powerful gods. Billy caught passing impressions of them; humans with grotesque animal heads. A lioness, a crocodile and a jackal...

Billy staggered. The vision was so strong that it felt as if his head was full of bricks, so heavy that he couldn't stand. He stumbled and collapsed back into the chair.

He tried to stand and fell almost immediately, tumbling forwards this time, but he managed to get his hands out and stop his face from hitting the floor.

Wellington licked Billy's cheek. If the wave of magick hadn't woken him, the dog's bad breath definitely would have done the job. His face was now level with the glass eyes of the tiger-skin rug. Billy blinked...

The tiger moved.

Billy blinked again, trying to decide what was real and what was an after-effect of the vision. The tiger was definitely moving, but it wasn't coming alive. The tiger-skin rug was moving because something was *underneath* it.

A hump appeared in the middle of the tiger's back, and as Billy watched the hump grew. It was terrifying to see. Billy wanted to run away, but that was not what S.C.R.E.A.M. detectives did. Slowly the hump grew bigger, rising up off the ground and taking the tiger rug with it. Two other lumps emerged on either side of the first hump. A head and two shoulders, pushing the animal skin upwards.

As the carpet rose, Billy could see a swirling circle of sand. He recognized that he had seen the same effect before, at the railway station when they first arrived.

It was as if there was a tiny tornado, driving the sand in dizzying circles. And appearing out of that magical circle – seemingly rising up from the floor – was the mummy.

So that was the secret of the sand circles! They were magick doors. *That* was how the mummy got in without breaking any windows or doors and how a burglar as conspicuous as a mummy was able to make a clean getaway without any witnesses. Charley would be fascinated. He only hoped that he lived long enough to tell her.

The mummy had fully emerged now in all its ragged glory. It towered over Billy, dominating the room. Billy already knew the raw power in those undead arms. There wasn't a second to lose.

Brave Wellington was already on the attack. The terrier had sunk its teeth into the mummy's leg. Billy grabbed the cricket bat and took a mighty swipe at the mummy's head. He'd once hit a ball for six and he desperately wanted to do it again. Billy put all of his strength into the swing and the mummy's head rocked on its shoulders.

The creature paused for a second. Its head was at an impossible angle, but with a sound of clicking bone, it righted itself again. The mummy gave a furious groan and lunged at Billy. It grabbed him by the lapels of his jacket and threw him across the room, kicking Wellington after him. Then it turned its attentions to the safe.

"*Nnnnnnnnnngggggggggghhhhhhhhhhhhhhhhh.*"

Billy fell in an ungainly heap in the corner, followed swiftly by Wellington, who landed with a yelp. It was time to get out the big guns, literally. Calling on all his inner calm, Billy picked up the blunderbuss and levelled it at the mummy. It was a crude weapon, a type of shotgun which fired a single massively destructive charge. Aiming carefully, Billy pulled the trigger. A huge muzzle flare leaped from the barrel as the shot ripped a hole through the mummy's torso. Billy's ears rang. The air was filled with the smell of gunpowder, stronger even than the mummy's graveyard stink.

The mummy swayed back on its heels, almost thrown to the ground by the sheer explosive force of the blast. But not quite.

The blunderbuss had done hideous damage. Billy could see right through the wound and out the other side. It was a ragged hole, but nowhere near as distressing as if the victim had actually been a living creature. The mummy bled only dust and sand.

The mummy howled, more in anger than in pain. But it did not stop.

It stomped over to the safe, twisted the door off its hinges and begun to stuff handfuls of jewels into a leather bag across its shoulder. Billy caught a flash of brilliant red – the Phoenix Egg that the Sandman needed for his potion of immortality.

When the safe was empty, the mummy raised its arms and advanced on Billy. Billy hurled the empty blunderbuss at the monster but it bounced off the mummy's chest. Billy attacked again with the cricket bat as Wellington fearlessly went for the monster's legs. He had to try to stop those cloth-bound hands before they reached his neck – but it was useless. He was trapped in the corner of the room with no way out and no way to stop the creature from killing him.

In the distance, he heard a commotion of footsteps and a voice which he recognized. Inspector Diggins had arrived! But it was too little, too late. With a hideous growl, the mummy lurched towards Billy and flung both arms around him in a rib-breaking embrace, picking him up as if he were just a doll.

The magical gateway swirled into life again as the mummy carried Billy into the vortex of sand. Wellington raced after them, sinking his teeth into the hem of Billy's trousers in an attempt to hold him back.

But the dog failed.

Billy and the mummy plunged into the eye of the sandstorm, and the world around them disappeared. Billy felt his entire body being wrenched out of reality by the magick door; it was as if he was being torn apart by the desert winds. He thought that he might have been screaming, but he couldn't hear anything above the raging of the sand.

CHAPTER TWENTY-SIX

PRISONER OF THE GODS

Billy regained consciousness. He was lying on his back and realized with terror that he had been placed in an open coffin. He tried to sit up, but couldn't; his body felt stiff, his arms and legs wouldn't obey him. Perhaps it was a side effect of travelling through the sand circle? He attempted to flex his fingers and failed. He tried to call out but his voice was muffled by something...

Finally Billy understood what was wrong: he couldn't move because his arms were secured across his chest. He couldn't speak because his lips were lost beneath the folds of grave clothes. He'd been bound from head to toe in linen bandages. Only Billy's eyes were free. Free to panic. Free to be afraid.

Billy pushed those emotions down. He needed to keep a clear head if he was going to get out of this.

Over the sound of blood pounding in his ears, Billy could hear voices chanting – low words, filled with dark intent. There was also the mummy's unmistakable moan. But one voice rose above them all, a voice full of anger and authority. It was disturbingly familiar. He had to see!

Billy strained against his bandage wrappings, tugging and heaving against his bonds until they loosened enough for him to prop himself up on his elbows. Lifting his head above the lip of the coffin, Billy saw that he was in the temple from his vision. He searched for the owner of that angry voice and found him sitting on a golden throne.

You.

The Sandman was exactly how Angry Annie had described him. Tall, lean, with an angular face and dark eyes outlined in thick black make-up. The shaven head glistened in the flickering torchlight. Billy swallowed hard. He had seen the Sandman before. Spoken with him. Slept in the same house as him. Even though the Sandman was wearing flowing white robes instead of a black suit, bow tie, white shirt and gloves, there was no mistaking the man.

Billy felt furious with himself for missing the clues. He couldn't believe that he had been tricked by such a simple disguise. Billy spotted what looked like a large grey rat squatting beside the throne. That was no rat, it was Cowley's wig! Not a hair out of place!

Sir Gordon's butler had been working against them from the very start. And now Billy was completely at his mercy.

Cowley was not alone. The strange creatures from Billy's vision stood silently before the Sandman's throne. They wore the same elegant robes as Cowley but their heads shone like gold. Part human, part monster; all terror. They cast fearsome shadows up the temple walls; a lioness, a crocodile and a jackal. The gods of Egypt. What had Charley said they were called? Ah yes, Sekhmet, Sobek and Anubis. These were the monsters Billy had seen in his vision.

Billy shuddered. The Sandman was more powerful than they had possibly imagined if he had three gods of ancient Egypt at his command. This was going to be a lot harder than catching a pixie or charming a mermaid.

"Come!" Cowley commanded, clapping his hands

and summoning the mummy. Obediently the mummy shuffled forwards, carrying the leather satchel that it had stashed Lord Wintersfall's treasures in. The hole that Billy had blasted through the creature had not healed and thin traces of sand continued to drip from it like blood.

Cowley held out his hands and the mummy opened the satchel and poured out its contents. Gold necklaces, gold earrings, gold bracelets, pearls, diamonds and rubies came spilling out. So many jewels that Cowley couldn't hold them all and they overflowed onto the stone temple floor. Last of all came the massive ruby known as the Phoenix Egg.

Sekhmet, Anubis and Sobek drew near and bowed their heads to their master.

Sobek the crocodile whistled. It was a strangely human sound, Billy thought, and it was followed by some very human words. "Slap my leg and call me Susan," said Sobek. "This is even better than the last time."

Sekhmet the lioness shuffled a bit and the Sandman glowered at her. "Don't you give me that look," said Sekhmet, her voice oddly muffled. "I've been standing up for ages...and this headdress weighs a ton."

199

"She's right," chipped in Anubis. "How come *you* get the chair every time?"

"We've been through this before," snapped Cowley.

"Are we going to be much longer, do you think?" asked Sobek. The crocodile god fished inside his white robe and pulled out a pocket watch, holding it up to the eyeholes of what Billy now saw was a golden mask. "Time really is getting on, and I'll be in terrible trouble if I don't get back in time for my morning duties."

So they aren't really gods at all, Billy realized with relief. Cowley's accomplices were just humans. *Evil* humans in fancy dress.

Cowley shot to his feet, his bald head glistening, anger flashing across his face. "Enough of your snivelling!" he roared. "We are in this *together*...but never forget that it was *my* knowledge, *my* efforts and *my* plan that brought us this far!" He slumped back down, his chest rising and falling with emotion.

When he spoke again his voice was back under control. "Surely none of you want to turn away now? Think of the rewards for one small sacrifice."

"What are you on about?" asked Sobek the crocodile. "What sacrifice?"

"Human sacrifice," hissed the Sandman, his voice

dripping with malice. "Our meddling young police officer over there has poked his nose in one too many times."

It hit Billy like a steam train, knocking all the air from his lungs. *That's me Cowley's talking about. He's going to cut out* my *heart to make himself immortal!*

"*Human sacrifice!*" spluttered Sobek the crocodile. Or rather, said the man inside the stuffy crocodile mask. "You're going too far, Cowley. We never talked about killing anyone."

Sekhmet the lioness and Anubis the jackal made noises of agreement. Cowley said nothing, although his fists clenched and unclenched on the arms of his golden throne.

Sobek continued. "When we started this scheme, you said that we could get our own back and I was fine with that. But this new plan of yours is too much. Killing a police officer…? We can't."

"I agree," said Sekhmet. "Lady Tiffin is a right old cow and I wanted to make her suffer a bit, but there's a difference between stealing stuff and murder! We'll all be hanged."

Anubis the jackal chipped in. "I'm in it for the money, plain and simple. I thought that was what this was about, making us rich. I never really understood why we have to wear these fancy-dress costumes that you're so keen on, and I have no intention of continuing with your crackpot scheme. I'll take my share of the jewels, thank you very much, then I'm packing my bags and I'm on the first train out of Edinburgh."

"I'm with you," Sobek the crocodile agreed. "I've had enough of this."

Cowley broke his silence with a whisper, somehow more powerful, more terrifying than any shout. "You are going nowhere," he rasped. "You ungrateful imbeciles."

"Just try and stop me," said Anubis. "Come on," he urged the other two. "Let's leave him to it."

"You really don't understand, do you?" said Cowley, fingering his gold necklace. "I wear the Eye of Horus, I control the mummy and this isn't over until *I* say it's over."

Anubis made a dash for the door, half stumbling over the hem of his white robe in his rush to be free of Cowley and his madness.

"*Stop him!*" Cowley ordered his undead servant. The mummy jerked into life. The bandage-wrapped head snapped round, eyeless gaze locking on Anubis. The jaw twitched and the mouth snapped, yellow teeth clacking together, like an insane clockwork toy. Then the arms rose and the mummy staggered across the chamber on stiff legs, slowly at first but gaining momentum with each step.

Anubis paused for a fraction of a second, as if sheer terror was stopping his feet from doing what his brain was surely screaming for them to do – *run, idiot!* By the time he came to his wits, the mummy was already upon him. Billy flinched as he witnessed those cloth-wrapped hands reach out and grasp Anubis by the neck. Cowley laughed.

Billy saw the chance to try to make his own escape while Cowley and his accomplices were distracted. Inside the confines of the open coffin he struggled against his linen bandages like a stage escapologist, doing everything he could to try to get loose. Out of the corner of his eye, Billy could still see Sekhmet and Sobek shrinking back in fear as the mummy started to crush the life out of their partner in crime.

Cowley continued to laugh. The mummy continued to strangle.

"Stop it," said Sobek. *"Please."*

Anubis was struggling violently, but nothing could break the grip of the mummy's cold, dead hands. Awful gagging, gasping sounds escaped from inside his golden mask.

"You've made your point," pleaded Sekhmet. "Now let him go, for pity's sake."

Cowley ignored her whimpering.

The mummy lifted Anubis off the ground by his neck as if he weighed no more than a child. Sekhmet looked away. Billy guessed she couldn't bear to watch the thrashing legs or hear the final gasps...

"Release him," Cowley finally ordered with a clap of his hands. Anubis fell to the ground, wheezing and writhing in pain.

"You worms," growled Cowley. "You pathetic, snivelling, spineless, gutless worms. Kneel before me!"

Gasping for breath, Anubis managed to crawl across the flagstone floor until he was sprawled in front of Cowley's throne. Sekhmet and Sobek joined him there on their knees, their heads bowed in defeat.

"Are you crying, love?" whispered Sekhmet, as snivels echoed from inside the crocodile mask.

"Yes," Sobek admitted, "and I can't get a hanky inside this bloomin' thing. There's snot everywhere in here."

"Silence," Cowley hissed. "You can serve me willingly, or you can serve me as slaves, but you *shall* serve me.

The mummy obeys only me and if you are stupid enough to still think that you might be able to outrun or hide from our undead friend here, then I have other ways to bring you to your knees." Gloating, Cowley revealed three tiny wooden coffins that had been concealed beneath his throne. In each coffin was a wax figure. One had a fingernail for a smile, one had a cufflink pressed into its wax chest, one was bound in a length of yellow ribbon.

"You know what these are, don't you?"

The fake gods nodded meekly.

"You recognize the totems as belonging to you, don't you?"

"That's my hair ribbon," said Sekhmet. "I thought I'd lost it."

"And I found it," Cowley crowed. "So anytime you get foolish ideas into your heads – ideas like…ohhh, I don't know…betraying me to the police, or running away, or trying to wriggle your way out of our partnership – then all I have to do is take one of my little wax dollies here and…well, what could I do?" A malicious smile crept across his lips. "I could throw it into a fire and watch it bubble away into nothing, or pull its arms and legs off, or bury it so deep that no one would ever find it.

Does any of that sound like something you might enjoy?"

Sobek and Sekhmet shook their heads. Anubis kept his face to the floor. Billy listened, still working on his gag. *Nearly there.*

"I thought not. So, back to where we started before I was so rudely interrupted. I almost have everything I need," Cowley continued. He held up a bottle, pulled out the cork and sniffed the contents, flinching at the rancid smell that wafted out. "Milk from a black cow..." He pulled a small, furry object out of a pouch beside the throne. "The paw of a white cat..." A twisted vegetable came next, a root which had the appearance of a gnarled, misshapen man. "Mandrake root." He rattled a handful of money. "Coins from a dead man's purse. And, of course, the Phoenix Egg... Now all I need is my final ingredient. A human heart – is that too much to ask?"

Billy finally managed to spit out his gag. "It depends who you're asking!"

"Oh, Master Flint," said Cowley. "So glad you could join us. It would be awful if you were to sleep through your starring role."

Cowley stalked over until he was standing beside

the coffin, looking down at Billy. "You and your girlfriend think you've been so clever, don't you, interfering with my plans? By the time I'm finished with you, you'll wish you never escaped my scorpion."

Billy wanted to say something witty, but fear had turned the words in his mouth to dust.

Cowley flicked his razor-sharp hippo-tusk wand back and forth over Billy's chest. It had been sharpened to a lethal point. "One quick slice, and I will have everything I need to walk into eternity."

"Make it quick then," said Billy, with more courage than he felt. "I'm getting bored of the sound of your voice. All power-hungry lunatics sound the same to me."

"You'd better get used to it," said Cowley, "because once I've got your heart, I have other plans for your body. Sobek, Sekhmet, Anubis, fetch the wax!"

Obediently Cowley's minions brought over a cauldron of wax supported on a metal tripod, with a brazier of hot coals beneath it. Billy could hear the contents bubbling explosively. Careful not to spill the red-hot wax, Sekhmet and Anubis removed the brazier and positioned the tripod and cauldron so that it hung over Billy's coffin. This close Billy saw that the cauldron had a lip so that its contents could be poured...over him!

CHAPTER TWENTY-SEVEN

THE MUMMY'S REVENGE

"So remind me again why you've covered my conservatory floor with sand?" said Sir Gordon.

"We're making a door," said Charley. "A magical gateway that will allow us to travel instantly from one place to another. Or I think it will, anyway."

Doogie had fetched a bag of sand from the garden. Charley instructed him to pour out a circle and now was busy writing in it with a bamboo cane. She had been staring at the hieroglyphs for so long that she could have written them blindfolded. "As far as I can tell," she said, "all I have to do is enter the circle and…"

"And what?" said Doogie.

"If I'm right, I'll be transported to the Sandman's lair."

"And if you're wrong?"

"Then I might be lost for ever inside a magical tunnel over which I have no control." Charley rubbed her legs. She was tired, and she was worried about Billy. Her back burned like fire. Same old, same old. There was a hard knot of fear in the pit of her stomach too; she had no idea what she would find at the other end of the magick circle. But Charley also felt excited; the same as every police officer does when they were closing in on their suspect. "I'm going through the gateway," she said firmly. "This ends now."

Charley drew her gun from under her blanket. Then she wheeled into the circle and waited for the magick to begin.

And she waited.

Then she waited some more.

"Something's wrong," she said, wondering whether she had copied the hieroglyphics correctly. She looked down and spotted the problem – the wheels of her chair had broken the circle. "Can you pass me the stick again, please, Doogie."

Doogie gave her the bamboo cane and Charley redrew

the circle with a flourish. "There!" she said, letting the cane drop and holding her pistol ready for whatever was waiting for her. Instantly the magick circle began to activate. "Goodnight, boys," she said as the vortex began to swirl around her. The sand flew round at incredible speed and Charley had the sense that she was in the middle of a desert storm.

Unexpectedly a hand burst through the swirling wall. "I'm comin' with ye, miss," said Doogie, stepping into the magick circle with her.

"Doogie! That was stupid of you!" Charley snapped. "You could have been torn in two, standing half in and half out of the portal!" Her voice softened. "Stupid, but very brave."

The whirlwind surrounded them completely. Charley caught a fleeting flash of white above her head and as some loose feathers began to spin around them, Charley realized that Queen Victoria had flown into the gateway too. Honestly, was there anyone who *wasn't* coming? Oh yes. Sir Gordon. She could just make him out through the blizzard of sand...he was waving...then he totally disappeared from view.

Charley became aware that the conservatory had vanished too. It wasn't just hidden behind the wall of sand – it had gone. Beyond the vortex there was only a sea of black stretching in every direction. As vast as the ocean. As high as the sky. Doogie reached out and grabbed her arm, more for his comfort than for hers she suspected. Charley clenched her revolver even more firmly as the portal took them deeper into the darkness. There was no up any more, no down. Just emptiness for ever...

Except that it wasn't really empty. Charley had worked for S.C.R.E.A.M. for long enough to know that the spiritual realm – whatever you wanted to call it – was real. Just as real as the flesh-and-blood, bricks-and-mortar world. Angels and demons and *things* all existed. She had seen some of them. Shot some too. And this magick door that the Sandman had created was taking them on a shortcut via one of those spirit realms.

Charley had no idea how long they had been travelling. It might have been a split second or a thousand years. She was pleased that Doogie had been foolish enough to come with her now. And even more pleased when the sandstorm started to slow.

It was only then that Charley spotted the terrible fault in her plan. She had completed the magick circle having *no idea* where it would take her. Was she going to find herself back at Lady Tiffin's house or Lavinia Fitzpatrick's front room? Charley's *theory* was that each crime scene had *two* portals – an entrance and an exit – and that the "exit" sand circle led directly to the Sandman's lair. Wherever that might be. But it was still just a theory.

The vortex was beginning to thin and Charley squinted through the sand as she tried to make out where they had materialized. "Definitely not Lady Fitzpatrick's," she breathed, as she took in their surroundings. Tall pillars supported a roof which had been painted to look like the night sky. Blazing braziers provided a flickering light which glinted off a golden throne and three animal-headed gods. They had landed in an Egyptian temple.

"Jings," gasped Doogie, brushing at the sand that covered them both. "I guess we're not in Scotland any more."

"Shhhh," Charley warned, all of her police instincts tingling. They were seriously outnumbered here.

Charley still held her pistol in front of her. There were five possible targets and six bullets in the chamber. Squinting along the barrel, Charley quickly passed over the mummy – who hadn't been stopped by bullets the last time. There were three gods in a row, Sobek, Sekhmet and Anubis – what good would bullets be against them?

She let her aim rest on a bald man who matched the description of the Sandman. He was holding a knife which he seemed intent on plunging into Billy, who – she realized to her horror – was tied up and helpless in a coffin. Charley levelled her gun and took aim; she'd soon put a stop to that!

At this range the mysterious Sandman seemed oddly familiar. Although she could only see the back of his head, the villain looked remarkably like Mr Cowley. Charley could slap herself for not having realized sooner – it was so obvious now! She held the gun a little tighter, her finger hovering on the trigger.

Charley squinted down the barrel of her pistol...she wouldn't kill Cowley, but she *could* shoot the knife from his hand. What might happen after that was anybody's guess. The only thing that was on their side right now was the element of surprise—

"*We are not amused!*" shrieked Queen Victoria as she flapped around the temple, ruining everything. Charley toyed with the idea of shooting the blasted bird instead.

The Sandman turned to face her. "We meet again, Miss Steel."

"Mr Cowley," said Charley. "So it's true what they say. It really is hard to get good staff nowadays..."

She eased back on the hammer and cocked her gun. "Now put the dagger down, *slowly*—"

"Or what?" Cowley challenged, still brandishing the bone knife above Billy. "Don't just stand there, you imbeciles!" He snapped his fingers at his henchmen. "Get them! She's just a girl playing at being in the police – she wouldn't dare—"

Charley pulled the trigger as the three gods rushed towards her. She dared all right.

Click!

The gun didn't fire. Charley pulled the trigger again. Another click. *It was jammed.*

"The mechanism is clogged with sand, I imagine," said Cowley, gloating. "The gateways are swift, but they aren't the cleanest form of travel."

With a very unladylike cuss, Charley hurled her useless weapon at the nearest attacker. It hit the crocodile-headed god squarely in the face, leaving a dent in his mask. *Not immortal after all*, she thought with a smirk, and more than a little relief.

Sekhmet the lioness made a grab for Doogie, who ducked and swung his best punch, catching Sekhmet in the pit of the stomach. Sobek the crocodile was closing in on Charley. She backed away as fast as she could, but without her gun there wasn't much she could do – Sobek was bigger and stronger. He clutched her by the shoulders, squeezing so hard that Charley could feel her skin bruising. Doogie threw a few more wild punches, but Sekhmet overwhelmed him, holding the boy from behind in a crushing bear hug.

It was all over in seconds. They were prisoners of the Sandman.

"I gave you a chance to run away," said Cowley. "I warned you on the train. I sent Sobek to frighten you off at the station –" he glowered at the crocodile – "fat lot of good that was." Sobek lowered his head, acknowledging his rather pathetic attempt.

"You're all mad," said Billy, sitting up in the coffin but still bound hand and foot. "You know that, don't you?"

"Is it mad to dream of having the power of the gods to command? To be the immortal leader of an army of the undead?"

"Frankly, yes," said Charley crisply. "As mad as a sackful of badgers."

"But I *can* make it happen, Miss Steel. Who do you think read all those books about Egyptology? Who decided the location of the archaeological dig which unearthed my cloth-bound friend here? Sir Gordon

Balfour, that bumbling idiot? No! It was me! All me! And what reward did I get for my troubles? More than five thousand gold items came out of that dig, and what did His Lordship give me as a thank you?" He waved his hippo-tusk wand. "A single piece of ivory… Little did the fat fool know the power that it held."

"You'll never get away with this, you despicable little man," said Charley.

"Oh, that's right, Your Ladyship, don't forget to keep stepping on the servants. You and Sir Gordon come straight out of the same mould." Cowley was almost spitting. "You think you're so much better than me, don't you?"

"That's not what I meant," Charley protested.

"*I* think I'm better than you," said Billy defiantly, as he continued to wrestle with his bonds, twisting back and forth. He wasn't going to give up without a fight. He had spotted a rack on the far wall beside Cowley's throne which held bows and arrows, swords with broad sickle-shaped blades, and a large axe with a curved head which splayed out on both sides like a fan. *If I can get my hands on them…*

"Why so cruel, young Master Flint? Have a heart… Wait a minute, why don't I have yours?"

Suddenly, the woman disguised as a lioness released her grip on Doogie. "I can't be part of this any longer," she said, her hands lifting off her heavy metal mask and throwing it to the ground. "I don't care what you do to me, I'm out."

It was Lady Tiffin's unhelpful housekeeper, Mrs Whisker! Charley recognized her immediately. She never forgot a hairy lip.

"Mrs Whisker!" said Cowley, glaring at her. "Put your mask back on at once."

The snivelling crocodile also removed his headpiece and let it clatter to the floor. "I'm finished too."

"Harris," said Billy, remembering how those cold eyes had looked down on him when they first met. "What would Lady Fitzpatrick say?"

"'You're fired,'" said Harris, hanging his head in shame.

Billy stared at Cowley's final follower and his detective brain told him who was hiding behind the jackal mask. It could only be Lord Wintersfall's servant. The butlers did it! "Come out, Mr Humble. I know you're in there."

"ENOUGH!" Cowley bellowed. "If you miserable dogs don't have the courage to stand with me, then you are against me." He turned to the mummy. "Kill them all!"

The mummy raised both arms and lurched forwards. Harris and Whisker almost fell over each other in a scramble to climb the three stone steps that led to the door. They were quickly followed by Humble, who ditched his jackal mask and hitched up the hem of his robe. "Wait for me!"

Together they put their backs to the stone door. With their combined strength, multiplied by their adrenaline-fuelled fear, the huge slab began to shift.

Looking out through the open door, Charley got a first sense of their location. From the rows of stone crosses and headstones outside, it seemed that the tomb they were in was situated in a gloomy graveyard. Harris, Whisker and Humble blundered through the gravestones and ran as if their lives depended on it – which they did.

Charley wanted to get out too, but the only way she would leave this chamber was with Billy and Doogie at her side. The mummy marched towards her with surprising speed, as if the withered muscles were growing stronger – perhaps it was Cowley's power as a magician that was growing instead. Charley wheeled backwards as fast as she could, positioning a pillar between her and the mummy while searching for something she could use as a weapon to fight the creature off.

"*God save me!*" yelled Queen Victoria.

Me too, thought Charley.

"Quick," Charley whispered to Doogie. "Have you still got that knife tucked down your sock?"

"Aye," said Doogie. "A true Scot always knows where his dirk is."

"Well get it out quick," she hissed, "and get Billy free!"

While Doogie headed towards Billy, Charley did what she could to distract Cowley and keep the mummy at bay.

The mummy had got closer than she'd realized and she had to duck as its massive fist swept over her head and buried itself in a pillar, sending up a cloud of dust. Charley spun her chair round and weaved between the pillars on the left-hand side of the temple…while Doogie made his way towards Billy on the right.

Cowley, meanwhile, was starting to panic as his schemes began to crumble around him. "Kill her!" yelled Cowley to his mummy servant. "Kill them all!"

The mummy followed Charley relentlessly, and she had no doubt she would be the one to get tired first. But Charley also knew that mummies had their brains removed by having a metal hook inserted up their nose.

Her brain was very much where it should be. She *should* be able to outwit it!

Charley made a feint to the left, and when the mummy lurched in that direction, she darted to the right. She edged towards one of the flaming braziers filled with burning coals. It was just low enough for her to reach. Using her blanket to protect her hands from the scorching heat, Charley picked up the dish, and hurled it at the mummy like a discus.

Cowley roared in anger as he saw the missiles fly towards his bandage-wrapped slave. Queen Victoria shrieked as she flapped frantically to avoid the hailstorm of fire.

But the mummy was too quick. It swatted the spinning dish out of the air, sending it clanging against the temple wall. A few coals did strike home however, peppering the creature's bandages with red-hot embers. A dozen points or more on the mummy's body were on fire; but still it did not stop.

In all the confusion, Doogie scrabbled over to Billy and began to cut through the bandages. "Quicker!" hissed Billy.

Cowley was heading for them, his face full of thunder, dagger raised. "Oh no you don't!" he yelled.

"Last one," said Doogie, using his knife to saw through Billy's bandages. Billy leaped free from the coffin just as Cowley was upon them. The butler lashed out with his foot, sending the cauldron flying. Billy and Doogie threw themselves clear of the hot wave of wax which came bubbling and blistering across the floor towards them. A thousand drops of liquid pain splashed out. Billy glanced into the coffin, now a fatal bath of molten wax. *If I'd still been in there...*

Back on his feet, Billy's thoughts immediately went to the weapon rack next to the throne. Unfortunately Cowley read his mind.

"You want this, do you?" He lifted a brutal-looking double-bladed axe. "Come and get it, boy. But I warn you, I've been practising." Cowley twisted his wrist and began to spin the axe expertly. "All work and no play makes the butler a dull boy."

"Dull boy! Dull boy!" echoed Queen Victoria.

Without warning, the parrot swooped down towards Cowley. He flailed at the bird furiously, trying to fend it off. But Queen Victoria was quicker. With a triumphant caw, she snatched the Eye of Horus talisman that hung on a gold chain around his neck. There was a brief tug-of-war, the chain snapped and Queen Victoria flew off, the source of the Sandman's magical power held firmly in her beak.

"Get the Eye of Horus, Duchess!" Billy yelled. "It's how he controls the—"

Billy didn't get to finish his sentence. Cowley's axe whistled towards him, slicing the air. Billy flung himself face down and felt the whisper of the blade as it just missed his head.

Still following Cowley's last command to *kill them all,* the mummy was now relentlessly stalking after Doogie. Though the lad had his knife ready, he was paralysed with fear. The mummy swept Doogie's blade aside with one blow and grabbed him in a death grip.

Cowley swung his axe again, but Billy managed to snatch a hook-bladed sword from the rack and block the blow. Sparks flew as Cowley's axe clanged against Billy's sword.

"This is going to be fun," sneered Cowley, raising his axe and raining down blow after blow. It was all that Billy could do to fend them off.

Doogie, meanwhile, was turning a shade of beetroot red as the mummy squeezed the life out of him, the bandaged arms crushing the lad's ribcage.

Charley had set her sights on Queen Victoria and the

Eye of Horus, but the stupid bird had found a place to perch near the top of one of the pillars. The parrot was fascinated by the talisman and showed no sign of wanting to come down.

"Sorry, Your Majesty," said Charley, dragging her shoe off her foot and then throwing it straight at the bird. Queen Victoria dodged her missile but she also dropped the pendant. *Yes!*

Cowley saw it fall too and dived for it. Billy grabbed Cowley's legs in a rugby tackle and they fell in a tangled heap. But Cowley's grasping fingers were nearly there… "It's mine I tell you. MINE!"

But his victory was cut short when Charley rolled her wheelchair over his outstretched hand and picked up the pendant for herself.

"The Eye of Horus," said Charley, recognizing one of the most potent symbols in Egyptian magick. Tying a quick knot in the broken chain she slipped the necklace over her head. "Oh lovely," she said, "it fits."

Doogie was gasping for breath as the mummy continued to crush him remorselessly.

Charley raised her hand to the mummy. *"Stop!"*

Obediently the mummy froze.

"Release the boy."

224

Again the mummy obeyed.

"No," Cowley shrieked. "*I* am your master!"

The mummy growled at Cowley but refused to move.

"You obey ME!" Cowley was screaming now. "I brought you back to life, you are my servant, MINE!"

Charley wondered what order she should give the mummy. Kill Cowley? No, she was a police officer, not an executioner. Capture Cowley?

Charley allowed herself a smile as she came up with a different idea. Being a servant had driven Cowley down such a desperate and bitter path of revenge, so perhaps...?

"I give you one last command," said Charley. "I set you free from whatever chains you have been bound with."

The mummy started to roar. "Fffffeeeeeerrrrrrrrrr." Its head snapped round so that it was facing Cowley. It took a slow step towards its former master. Then another.

Cowley laughed. "See," he sneered. "The mummy is my slave...and always will be."

"Fffffffffeeeeeerrrrrrrrrrreeeeeeeeeeeeee," groaned the mummy, standing in front of Cowley.

It placed one hand on Cowley's shoulder. Then the other.

"Fffffferrrreeeeeeee," said the mummy. "Ffrree."

The mummy's hands began to squeeze Cowley's shoulders. Charley watched the emotions change on Cowley's face. Confusion becoming fear becoming pain.

Cowley wasn't finished yet, however. With a massive show of force, he took his axe in both hands. Clenching the shaft and using it like a quarterstaff he pushed up and away, breaking the mummy's death grip. Without even pausing, Cowley let one hand slide along the shaft and brought the axe down with a mighty *chop*.

The mummy looked at the stump where his arm had been. Then he looked down at his bandaged feet where the severed arm lay. "Freeeee," the mummy growled, swinging his one remaining fist at Cowley's head. On the floor, the detached arm jerked towards Cowley's legs, snatching at his ankles and dragging a trail of loose bandages behind it.

Cowley attacked again. This time the axe connected with the mummy's neck, slicing through the corpse like butter. The mummy's head bounced across the floor to land at Billy's feet.

But the headless body and the disconnected arm continued to attack.

"Freeee," said the mummy's severed head.

Billy picked it up. "Here you go, mate," he said, tossing it to Cowley. "Catch!"

Cowley caught the head instinctively. As he held it in his hands more bandages uncurled. The leathery lips moved. "Free," the mummy gurgled. Then it tried to bite Cowley's fingers with its ancient brown teeth.

Charley and Doogie turned their attentions towards the door of the tomb and the outside world. A dog was barking in the distance – someone else was coming their way.

"Go, Doogie," said Charley, "get out while you still can."

Doogie looked at the three steep steps which led to the open door and freedom. He looked back at Charley. "I'll not leave ye, miss."

On impulse Charley took the young lad's hand and kissed it. "Go and get help," she said. "That's an order."

By now, Cowley had dropped the mummy's head on the floor and lifted his axe to split it in two. He would have managed it too if Billy hadn't stepped in behind him and grabbed him by the wrists. But Cowley was bigger and stronger than Billy and easily able to break the young detective's hold. With a callous grin, Cowley turned and kicked Billy in the stomach. Billy crumpled to the floor in pain.

The headless mummy was beginning to unravel completely, the bandages peeling away from the preserved body. The strips of cloth writhed in the air like the legs of an octopus, apparently with a life of their own...

Cowley raised his axe again, this time aiming for Billy.

"*Off with his head!*" shouted Queen Victoria.

"Nooooooo!" shouted Charley.

"Freeee," gurgled the mummy's head.

Whilst Charley watched, terrified, the animated bandages reached out. They looped around Cowley's wrists and pulled as tight as a hangman's noose. Other living bandages snatched the axe out of Cowley's grasp.

As Billy scrambled backwards on his hands and feet, every last strip of cloth unwound from the mummy. The bandages snaked out and lashed themselves around Cowley. He tried to escape but the bandages were too quick. First his legs were captured, rooting him to the spot. Then his arms, his body. His face.

It was a macabre sight. The mummy was gradually reduced to a walking headless skeleton, wizened brown muscles clinging to yellow bones, while Cowley was turned into a living mummy, screaming with every fresh binding that tightened around him.

Finally it was complete. The bodily remains of the mummy stood for a second – and then collapsed, disintegrating into dust. A grisly skull with leathery skin pulled tight against the bone was all that was left to show that the mummy had ever been there at all.

"Peace," sighed the mummy's skull and then his head too crumbled away into nothing more than sand.

The momentary silence was interrupted by the sound of footsteps like a herd of elephants, charging down the tomb steps. Wellington came first, a scrap of Billy's trouser leg still in his jaws. Doogie was a close second, followed by three burly constables manhandling three ashamed-looking servants, dressed in Egyptian robes. Inspector Diggins brought up the rear, bravely wielding a notepad and sharp pencil.

"Just as I suspected," Inspector Diggins declared, looking at Cowley who was struggling against his bandages. "I knew all along the bandages were a disguise."

LOOSE ENDS

After the dust had settled... After Charley had washed the last traces of sand from her hair... After the stolen jewels had been returned and 44 Morningside Place restored to what it considered to be "normal"... Charley and Billy were sitting quietly in the corner of the Last Drop Tavern.

Like in so many of their investigations before, the bizarre and the supernatural had been mixed up with an ordinary commonplace sort of crime in the case of the mummy's revenge. The Sandman, at the end of the day, was a servant with a grudge. And it had turned out that the Temple of the Seven Stars *was* located in a real tomb, but in Edinburgh, not ancient Egypt.

Rich men, like Lord Wintersfall, liked to look important even after they had died and spent fortunes building huge monuments in the cemeteries. This particular tomb, built in the Egyptian style, complete with carved palm trees on the front, was in The Grange cemetery, within sight of Lord Wintersfall's house. Inspector Diggins had found his way there, thanks to the persistence and keen nose of a very special Scottish terrier named Wellington, and a scrap of Billy's trousers which had given him just enough scent.

Inspector Diggins wasn't very interested in the truth of the case. He had his suspects safely under lock and key and that was all that mattered to him. He didn't want to hear any mumbo jumbo about mummies and Egyptian magick. Mrs Whisker, Mr Harris, Mr Humble and Mr Cowley wouldn't be seeing freedom for quite some time.

"We didn't get any credit again," said Charley with a sigh.

"What's new?" said Billy. "Anyway, we don't do it for that, do we? That's not what S.C.R.E.A.M. stands for."

"So what do we stand for, Billy Flint?"

"Truth and justice, Charlotte Steel," said Billy.

"Following the clues wherever they take us. Finishing the case no matter what."

"I suppose you're right, Billy," said Charley. "Remind me why you've brought us here?"

Billy smiled at his partner. "Do you remember the mummy's final word?"

Charley nodded. How could she forget? "Peace."

"Exactly," said Billy. "And peace is one thing that our vital witness hasn't known in a very long time. The case isn't closed until Angry Annie gets justice too."

The place was empty. Billy had even asked the barman to leave.

"Annabel," said Billy gently. "It's me, Billy."

The ghost girl announced her presence with an icy blast.

"Is she here?" Charley asked, shivering.

"She's here," said Billy.

"I didn't think you'd come back," said Annie.

"I promised," said Billy. "And I always keep my promises."

"Can you really help me?" said Annie.

"I can," said Billy.

Annabel's face lit up. Charley smiled too, as the room began to thaw. She knew that Billy was as good as his word.

"What do you need from me?" Annabel pleaded. "I'll do *anything*." There was a hint of desperation in her voice.

"Please," said Billy, "you don't need to earn your freedom. It's a gift." Ghostly tears welled in Annabel's eyes. "It's time for you to move on to a better place," said Billy. "If you want me to, I'd like to say a few words in Latin and then you'll be released from the chains that you've bound yourself in."

A light sparkled in Annabel's eyes, making them seem blue and clear for the first time, instead of grey and dead.

Billy began. The words he spoke had a beauty and music that was all their own.

Peace fell upon the Last Drop Tavern. Charley couldn't explain what she was experiencing. She felt safe, wrapped in a blanket of love. Accepted. Forgiven. Charley closed her eyes and it was a summer's day inside her mind. The warmth was all around her. She was running through a field, laughing. The sheer joy actually spilled over her lips and Charley laughed out loud. She opened her eyes, worried she had spoiled the moment somehow.

Billy was sitting there with a huge smile on his face.

"Has she gone?" asked Charley.

The answer came in the shape of a single white

feather, appearing out of nowhere and floating down towards them. "I don't understand," said Charley, picking the feather up and examining it.

"Neither do I," said Billy. "Wonderful, isn't it?"

THE END

IF YOU LOVED

THE MUMMY'S REVENGE

TURN THE PAGE FOR MORE THRILLS AND CHILLS
FROM ANDREW BEASLEY...

S.C.R.E.A.M

THE CARNIVAL OF MONSTERS

Roll up, roll up, if you dare, to Doctor Vindicta's Carnival!
Gasp at the dancing ghosts! Grimace at the creepy clowns!
Giggle in the hall of mirrors!
It's all harmless fun and frights…until a young boy
disappears. The police believe he's run away, but his sister
swears he was snatched by a monster.

Only the bravest detectives can arrest a demon:
Billy Flint and Charley Steel, AKA S.C.R.E.A.M.,
top-secret investigators of Supernatural Crimes, Rescues,
Emergencies and Mysteries.

Epic adventure awaits in...
THE BATTLES OF BEN KINGDOM

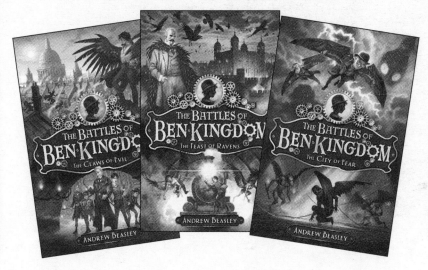

It is 1891 and London is at war. High up on the rooftops lives a ragtag band of orphans and spies – the Watchers – protectors of the city. Below the cobbled streets lurks the Legion, a ruthless gang of cut-throats and thieves, plotting to unleash the forces of HELL.

When a mysterious coin falls into his hands, street urchin, Ben Kingdom, is flung into the midst of this ancient battle. The fate of the world now rests with Ben, but which side will he choose? An army of angels...or the claws of evil.

ACKNOWLEDGEMENTS

Firstly, I want to thank Rebecca Hill for her unstinting support. Thanks also to Will Steele for his awesome design work and the brilliant Manuel Šumberac for his stunning cover. Special thanks, as always, go to the rather wonderful Anne Finnis; my first guide in the world of publishing. I must also mention Helen Greathead; I'll never forget your help.

As always, my pleasure in writing this book has been increased by the invaluable input from my talented editor, Stephanie King. Once again your instincts for a good story have steered me right, Stephanie. *Thank you.*

Special mention to my beloved Auntie Valerie on her 80th birthday – *bon anniversaire*!

Darling Jules; always and forever. Ben and Lucy; you are my heroes…you both get more incredible with every chapter. Thanks Ben for help with the acronym! Mum and Dad; I'm so proud of *you*. Mam and Jack; thanks for being there. Amanda; love you, sis.

Father; thank you for everything.

Some of you reading *The Mummy's Revenge* might have spotted your own name in the text. If you did, this means that I think you are a thoroughly super person. Alternatively it might mean that you just happen to sound like a servant or criminal. You know who you are!

ABOUT THE AUTHOR

Andrew Beasley was born in Hertfordshire, and has spent most of his life with his nose buried in a book.

As a student he read law in Bristol, but was disappointed to discover that life as a lawyer wasn't as exciting as books had led him to believe. He then spent a number of years travelling extensively across Europe for work, although he didn't see much of it because he was usually reading a book.

Andrew is now a primary school teacher, where he shares his passion for storytelling with his class. Andrew lives in Cornwall with his wife and their two children, Ben and Lucy.